The Ottery Lottery

by P.A. Nash

"The company I've built from nothing, Kennaway Coopers – well, I'm giving it away to the winner of the Ottery Lottery!"

Caleb Kennaway's family and the other board members violently disagreed with his decision. A month later, Caleb Kennaway was found dead at the foot of the main stairs in Kennaway Court.

The third book in the East Devon Cosy Mystery series finds Frank and Ella buying a ticket in the Ottery Lottery. This leads them into an opportunity to investigate Caleb's death and also a hunt for a miniature beer barrel that will change their lives.

Amongst the pages of The Ottery Lottery, you'll walk in pixies' footsteps, stumble into a tumbling weir, and discover granite poetry. Coupled with a plane crash and a Ptolemaic clock, there's a chance to reconnect with characters from Frank and Ella's recent past.

If you enjoy cosy mysteries set in the glorious English countryside, then join Frank and Ella on an easy-to-read adventure through the East Devon country town of Ottery St Mary as they seek to unmask the murderer of the man who ran the Ottery Lottery.

PA Nash has written a third delightful cosy mystery in which a mixture of two Agathas, Christie and Raisin, blend in with scenic local walks and landmarks. Once more, you'll be yearning to visit!

Copyright ©2019 by PA Nash.

All rights reserved. This book or any portion thereof may not be reproduced or used in any manner whatsoever without the express written permission of the publisher except for the use of brief quotations in a book review.

First Published 2019

www.eastdevoncosymysteries.com

Chapter One

*Since all that beat about in Nature's range,
Or veer or vanish; why should'st thou remain
The only constant in a world of change*

"Sometimes you make me want to kill you!" Christine screamed.

"The feeling's mutual." Caleb turned towards her, almost spitting out the words.

"Why? After all the hard work. Why?"

"Because it's my money and I want to have some fun with it."

"What about me?"

"You're well provided for. You always have been and you always will be."

"I don't understand you. I'm not sure I ever will!"

"Perhaps that's the problem."

Christine changed tack. "Doesn't Kenneth mean anything to you?"

"Yes, it's about time he stood on his own two feet."

"And Fabian and Carl? Have you told them? Don't they have a say?"

"Why do you think I asked them both to come here this evening? They're only directors. They can't outvote me. They'll do what I say. They always do."

A moment of silence descended upon the room as if they were preparing for the next onslaught. The calm before the storm.

There was a knock at the front door and Caleb went to open it.

"Come in, Fabian. Is Carl not with you?"

"No. Am I late?"

"You're never late. Come into the drawing-room and I'll pour you a drink."

Fabian followed Caleb into the room and sat down in one of the comfortable armchairs by the piano.

"Good evening, Fabian." A curt sharp voice greeted the man.

"Good evening, Mrs Kennaway." He would never dare to call her Christine.

Caleb brought Fabian his drink and handed another to Christine. She looked at him and for a moment, Caleb thought she might throw it back into his face.

"Where's Kenneth?"

"I'll call him," muttered Christine. She pulled out her mobile phone from her trouser pocket and dialled a number. "Kenneth, come down. We're almost ready to start."

Within half a minute they could hear the echo of footsteps on the stone stairs leading down into the front hall. There was another knock at the front door.

"I'll get it," a voice from the hall shouted.

"Good evening, Carl. We're in the drawing-room. Come through!"

Kenneth ushered the well-built man into the room. He was puffing and appeared out of breath. "Sorry, meeting finished a bit late."

"Sit down, Carl. Drink?"

"Yes, please."

After drinks had been dispensed and sipped, everyone sat down. Over the past few years, they each seemed to possess their allotted chair and drink. They all sat and drank as if in a trance. Caleb was the last to be seated. The rest of the room turned their eyes towards him. He had their undivided attention.

"I've brought you together this evening because I thought you deserved to hear the news, straight from the horse's mouth, as it were."

He smiled but no-one smiled back.

"I've decided to give up the chair and ownership of Kennaway Coopers. I'm retiring. I have enough money saved to keep on enjoying my lovely lifestyle, so I've…." He stopped to savour the moment.

"Oh, Caleb, stop messing around and tell them." Christine's voice stabbed into the expectant atmosphere.

"Alright, my dear." Caleb had a twinkle in his eyes and a smile upon his lips.

"I've already communicated this information with my wife. If you were anywhere in Ottery St Mary, you will have heard her reaction!"

He took a sip of his drink.

"Get on with it!" his wife snapped.

"I'm retiring and none of you will be taking my place as Chair or owner."

There was a sharp intake of breath from the gathered group.

"What do you mean?" blustered Kenneth.

"What I mean is that the company I've built from nothing, Kennaway Coopers–well, I will be giving it away."

There was an explosion of noise in the room.

Caleb held up his hand and shouted above the tumult. "I'm giving it away to the winner of the Ottery Lottery!"

 ༺༻

"Ladies and Gentlemen, members of the press. Welcome to Kennaway Court. I've invited you here this morning to announce the Ottery Lottery."

Four journalists stood in the drawing-room of Kennaway Court with notebooks and dictaphones in hand as Caleb Kennaway spoke.

"Over one year ago, I decided it was time to retire. Kennaway Coopers, makers of the famous Tar Barrels of Ottery is a thriving, dependable business. Under my tutelage, the company has a well-deserved reputation for reliable delivery, quality products and outstanding customer service. When I looked around at my potential successors, I could not honestly say that any of them could be trusted to continue to run the company to the same high standards."

The lady from the Ottery Gazette held up her hand. The other three were furiously scribbling. "Does you mean that Kennaway Coopers is closing down?"

"No, far from it. I hope it will continue to produce quality tar barrels for many years to come. I have a dedicated, skilled workforce. I have no wish to see them made redundant or out of work."

"Good," said the Gazette lady, "My husband has spent twenty years of his life working for you."

"I know, Rosemary, and I genuinely hope he has a job with the company for at least another twenty years. However, although the workforce may be first class, the same cannot be said for the rest of the management team!"

"Oh, Mr Kennaway, that's not very nice. Do you really want us to print that?"

"If you want to, I don't really care."

Caleb paused for breath.

"What I do care about is the Ottery Lottery. Let me explain. I will be selling tickets for the Ottery Lottery from this day onwards for one month only. During the next thirty days, anyone can buy a ticket. They are reasonably priced at £25 each. In one month's time, there will be a grand draw here at Kennaway Court and the winner of the Ottery Lottery will be the new owner and chair of Kennaway Coopers. The only stipulation I am going to make is that I would want the name of the company to remain the same."

The man from the Echo put down his pen and raised a hand. "So you're going to give the company away? For free?"

"Well, each ticket will cost £25. There will be no limits on how many tickets each person can buy."

"I assume you'll pocket the proceeds?"

"No. It's all going to go to a charity run by my wife. A charity that builds communes for orphaned children in Albania. It's called People's Orphanage Commune Albania. We call it POCA. But it's no gamble on our part. My wife receives no salary from the charity. Neither do I. Every pound raised will go to POCA. No top-slicing. No backhanders. All fair and above board."

"Talking of fair and above board. How can my readers be assured that this Lottery will be fair?"

"I have appointed a firm of solicitors from Budleigh Salterton to oversee the proceedings. I have given them full access to every meeting and every transaction."

A familiar figure walked into the room.

"May I introduce Alice Aylesbeare to you. She is the administrator at Buckerells of Budleigh. She may appear sweet and grandmotherly, but don't try to cross her. Her bite is much worse than her bark!"

Alice and Caleb fielded a few more questions before Caleb wrapped up the meeting.

"Thank you, everyone, for attending. Please publicise the Ottery Lottery far and wide. I look forward to meeting up with you again in one month's time."

☙❧

Frank and Ella Raleigh stood outside the white walls of Exeter Crown and County Court with a look of relief on both their faces. They had just emerged through the revolving door having completed their stint as witnesses in a murder trial. The local paper had labelled the case as the Dudleys of Budleigh and both Frank and Ella had played an important role in bringing the murderer to justice.

For now, they were desperate to travel back to their home in the sleepy town of Otterbury and continue their lives as retired school-teachers. In the past six months, they had become investigators in two cases of murder, they had been threatened, kidnapped and, on one occasion, Ella had been almost killed. Enough was enough. They agreed that it was time to go back to the quiet life.

As they were preparing to walk to their car, they heard a cry of "Oo-ee, Frank. Ella!" They turned around to see where it had come from and emerging from the revolving doors appeared Mrs Aylesbeare, the solicitor's secretary from Budleigh Salterton. Frank and Ella waited as a small well-rounded lady caught up with them. Ella was reminded of the first time they had met her. She was still wearing her ankle-length patterned woollen coat and a flowery hat–this time the hat was green in colour. As usual, she carried her large brown corduroy handbag. She still reminded

Frank of Miss Marple–straight from the pages of one of Agatha Christie's novels.

"Alice," called Ella, "have you finished as well?"

"Yes, but so has the trial. It took the jury so little time to come to their verdict."

"What was the verdict?"

"Guilty, of course. What else could it be?"

"Can we offer you a lift back to Budleigh?"

"No, it's OK. I've got my own car now. It's a 1979 Triumph Spitfire. Red, of course!"

"I didn't even know you could drive."

"Oh yes, ever since I was a young girl. I bought the car with my inheritance."

"Yes, of course. It's like you've won the lottery!"

All three of them began walking back to the car park on the other side of Magdalen Street.

"Speaking of the lottery," Alice said, "have you bought your ticket for the Ottery Lottery yet?"

"The what…?"

"The Ottery Lottery. I'd have thought you would have known all about it. It's in your part of the valley. You must have read it in the local paper?"

"No," said Ella, "we've been rather pre-occupied recently."

"Well, Caleb Kennaway who owns Kennaway Coopers is selling his company. They make the barrels that all the pubs in Ottery use on Tar Barrel Night. Why don't you pop into Ottery and get your ticket? You never know, you could be Kennaway Coopers next owner!"

They reached the car-park and both Frank and Ella nodded in admiration as Alice jumped into her Triumph Spitfire, revved up the engine and waved them farewell. The sound of the fiery red Triumph could be heard above the rest of the busy traffic as it made its way along Magdalen Street and off down the Topsham Road back to Budleigh.

⁂

Later that week, Frank and Ella drove into Ottery St Mary. With its parish church on the hill and its independent shops spreading out from the town square, the place had history. It had appeared in the Domesday Book. Its school, King's was a former grammar school founded by Henry the Eighth in 1545. The River Otter passed through the western edge of the town. Samuel Taylor Coleridge, he of the Ancient Mariner poem, was born in the town. It had Tar Barrel Night in November and Pixie Day in June. In 1866 the Great Fire of Ottery destroyed about a quarter of the town. In 1980 a commercial plane crashed landed in a nearby field narrowly avoiding the town. The only casualties were two sheep.

Ottery was not your bland, could-be-anywhere town.

Frank and Ella parked in the Canaan Way car park and made their way past the supermarket toward The Square. Ella stopped a middle-aged man loitering outside a hardware shop. "Excuse me, where do I buy my Ottery Lottery ticket?"

"Over there." He pointed at a trestle table set up on the road outside the council offices.

Sitting behind the table were two burly gentlemen, one dressed in a bright red cardigan and the other wearing a blue baseball cap with the words Kennaway Coopers emblazoned on it. They both stood up as Ella approached. "Good morning, how may we help you?" said the red cardiganed one.

"I'd like to buy a ticket for the Ottery Lottery."

"Not a problem. Each ticket costs twenty-five pounds. You can buy as many as you want."

"Thank you. Just one, please."

The baseball cap joined in. "You'll need to fill in this form. We'll need your name and a contact number. Just in case, you win."

The red cardigan continued the double act. "Also, please read the rules carefully. Every penny you spend on a ticket will be going to support the Commune Charity in Albania.

Baseball cap's turn. "There's a leaflet at the other end of the table describing all about the charity. Please take one if you wish."

Ella read and then filled in the form. She handed over her money which was promptly put away in a blue steel money box with the Kennaway logo stencilled across the lid.

"Do you both work for Mr Kennaway?" asked Ella.

"Yes, ma'am. We both left school on the Friday and started work at the Coopers on the next Monday. Didn't get a summer holiday that year." The blue baseball cap sounded proud and loyal.

"We're the senior workers, so we've been entrusted the task of selling these tickets. Also, we can check out our potential future boss."

"The only way you can buy a ticket is through us."

"You sound very organised. I'm most impressed."

"Thank you, ma'am." A small queue had built up behind Frank and Ella.

"Excuse us, ma'am, here's your ticket. Good luck."

Frank and Ella moved away and, seeing it was just after eleven o'clock, found themselves a local coffee shop in which they were happy to while away some time.

❧

Over in Kennaway Court, four people were discussing the events of the past week.

"I've been to see a solicitor In Exeter. He's allowed to do this. He can't be challenged."

"I'll challenge him. I'll put my hands around his throat and throttle him."

"That'll do no good. I bet he's changed his will."

"He's enjoying himself. I've never seen him look so happy and relaxed."

"I'm so angry with him."

"We all are!"

"We're sitting here talking. Isn't anyone going to take any action?"

"What sort of action."

"Extreme, drastic action."

Chapter Two

*And thus he sang: Adieu! adieu!
Love's dreams prove seldom true.*

The Ottery Lottery was the talk of the town for the next month. The trestle table appeared to be doing brisk business whenever Frank and Ella passed it by. The local newspaper and social media were full of background information and stories of what people would do with the company if they won.

Along with a great number of other ticket holders, Frank and Ella were pleased that their money was going to support what appeared to be a deserving charity. The Ottery Herald did a well-researched, in-depth series of articles on the charity called POCA. People's Orphanage Commune of Albania worked with a couple of orphanages in the capital of Tirana and at Sarandë on the coast near the Greek border. The money went into helping orphans receive schooling, a caring home and an opportunity to make a life for themselves.

"What would you do if you won, Ella?"

"I'd make sure the people of Ottery had a say in the company's future. I'd find someone with enthusiasm and vision to be the managing director and then I'd be a silent, sleeping partner."

Frank nodded in agreement. Life had returned back to its relaxing ways–walks with Betty and George, social gatherings in the village and absolutely no mixing with murder and mayhem.

Privately, both Frank and Ella admitted to themselves a touch of sadness that they were not involved in the quest for truth and justice, but they never shared their regrets with each other.

※

The day of the Ottery Lottery Draw was soon upon them and they made their way with multitudes of others to Ottery St Mary. The town was buzzing, the car parks were full, the coffee shops were doing a roaring trade. There were people excitedly gathered on every street corner. In the middle of the Square, PC Hydon was directing traffic. He gave Frank and Ella a wave when he saw them and almost caused an accident. Two lorries assumed his wave was permission for them to move forward. PC Hydon stopped them both just in time.

"Sorry!" he shouted as each driver shrugged their shoulders in gestures of dismay.

The Town Council had given permission for market traders to set up their stalls around the edge of The Square–something that had not occurred in the lifetime of many Ottery residents. Everything was alive. The chair of the Chamber of Trade was rubbing his hands in glee as he heard the continuous ting of cash registers all around the town.

The Draw for the Ottery Lottery was to be at 2 o'clock and so, after a rapidly consumed pre-booked lunch in the Volunteer Inn, Frank and Ella made their way up the hill, past the church, down College Lane, to Kennaway Court. The driveway was already filling up. There was an effervescent but respectful hum of conversation all around the grounds in front of the house.

"Don't the gardens look lovely?"

"I came last Sunday afternoon to have a good look around. The hydrangeas, the laurels and the Yew trees along by the follies were wonderful."

"Do they open up the grounds often?"

"Every Sunday afternoon for two hours. They charge but it's really worth it."

Frank and Ella found a place in the shade of one of the yew trees lining the west wall of the garden. People spilled off the paths and onto the lawns. The dry weather of the recent few weeks ensured that those lawns would not be decimated by the army of feet gathered on them. At five to two, several people emerged from the front door of Kennaway Court and stood at the top of the stone steps. Amongst them, Frank and Ella were surprised to see, Alice Aylesbeare.

"That's Alice! What is she doing there?" whispered Ella.

"Perhaps she's related to the family?"

At the foot of the steps was a wooden trestle table covered with a velvet effect cloth. On the cloth was positioned a small beer barrel, a large silver bowl complete with an ornate silver lid and a carved wooden bowl. There were microphone and loudspeakers set up on the wide stone steps that led up to the front door. At two o'clock an older looking, distinguished gentleman moved forward to the microphone.

"That be Caleb Kennaway," announced an old local standing alongside Frank and Ella.

Indeed, it was.

"Good afternoon, everybody. My name's Caleb Kennaway and I am the proud and present owner of Kennaway Coopers. I say present because, in a few minutes, I hope to pass on my ownership to the holder of the lucky ticket."

Caleb passed on the microphone to another man who was dressed in a dinner jacket and looked as if he was in charge of proceedings.

"Good afternoon, Ottery St Mary. I'm sure you know who I am – Richard Styles from Radio East Devon. Miles of smiles from Styles."

Those who recognised his catch-phrase smiled knowingly. The rest of the crowd awaited further information.

"Let me explain how the Grand Draw for the Ottery Lottery will work. In a short while, Mrs Kennaway will shuffle all the ticket-stubs and will draw out five tickets from the silver bowl. After that, Kenneth Kennaway, Mr and Mrs Kennaway's son, will draw the winning ticket from those five. Two observers from Buckerells of Budleigh will ensure that fair play is seen to be done."

A murmur of approval wafted around the crowd.

"That's why she's here," whispered Ella.

Richard Styles continued. "The winning ticket holder will be given this key. It will, I hope, open this miniature beer barrel." He moved to the table and held up a smart wooden barrel about a foot in height.

"This barrel was carved by Albert Fitzwarren. He was one of the first workers at Kennaway Coopers and now lives near Taunton. The work is Devon Ash, the carving includes symbolic representations of an otter, a pixie and the church of St Mary. The lid is kept in place with a brass hinge and a small brass lock and key. I have the key in an envelope in my pocket. The details about the ownership of Kennaway Coopers will be found inside the barrel."

This time there was a gentle round of applause. Somebody near the entrance shouted –"Get on with it."

Laughter replaced the applause.

"Thank you, Uncle Silas," chuckled Richard Styles. "So, without further ado, I call upon Mrs Kennaway to draw the five finalists."

Mrs Christine Kennaway stepped forward. She was dressed in a velveteen dark purple dress, edged with black. She wore black gloves and a black hat. She appeared as if she was going to a funeral.

Richard Styles held the microphone up to her face. "How are you feeling, Mrs Kennaway?"

"Like the rug has been pulled away from under my feet. This could be the worst day of my life, were it not for the fact that so much money will be going to my POCA charity.

"Make sure it does!" shouted out another wag from the back of the crowd.

"Oh, it will. Have no fear about that!" replied Mrs Kennaway.

Alice Aylesbeare went to the table and lifted the silver bowl. She gave the contents a vigorous shaking before she lifted off the lid.

Mrs Kennaway theatrically closed her eyes and put her left hand into the bowl. She withdrew it holding a folded ticket stub. Alice took the stub and handed it to Richard Styles.

"The first finalist is Sarah Barratt from Ottery St Mary."

Somebody near Frank and Ella cried "That's me!"

Mrs Kennaway and Alice repeated the procedure. Richard Styles called out. "James Spurway from Gittisham."

There was no cry of recognition this time.

Once again Mrs Kennaway put her hand into the box and once again Alice handed the folded stub to Richard Styles.

"Ella Raleigh from Otterbury."

"That's me!" cried Ella. All those in the immediate vicinity turned towards her and appeared pleased for her.

By now, the fourth name was ready to be announced.

"Christine Kennaway, from Ottery St Mary. I recognise that name!"

"I should think so too, considering how many tickets I bought."

"One more to go, Mrs Kennaway, please."

Alice put the lid back on the silver bowl and gave it another good shaking. She took off the lid, once more, and thrust the bowl in Mrs Kennaway's direction.

She reached in, in her exaggerated style, and pulled out the final ticket.

Alice handed over the ticket to Richard Giles who called out the final name. "My word, you did buy a lot of tickets. Mrs Kennaway, again!"

"Put it back!"

"Give someone else a chance!"

"Fix!"

The hecklers were in full voice.

Richard Styles held up a hand. "I'm referring this to our two observers."

There was a whispered huddle between Richard and the two observers from Buckerells. After a minute, Richard Styles turned back towards the gathered crowd.

"The two impartial observers have decided that the draw was done fairly, and the tickets drawn will stand."

There was more than a murmur as the crowd voiced a multitude of opinions to their nearest neighbours.

"I am going to place the five finalists into this splendid Radio East Devon wooden bowl, specially crafted for today by Windy Willow from nearby Aylesbeare. Thanks, Dick and Suzie!"

Richard Styles folded up the ticket stubs once more and dropped them into the bowl. He then placed his clipboard over the bowl and gave it all a most dramatic agitation.

"I call upon Kenneth Kennaway, son of Caleb and Christine Kennaway to put us all out of our misery and pull out the winning ticket."

The whole place went silent as Kenneth moved forward, rolled up his jacket sleeve and burrowed into the bowl. After a good swirl around for at least ten seconds, Kenneth grabbed a folded ticket stub and brought it out. Alice took it and handed it to Richard Styles.

He opened the ticket stub out and looked at the name. With a huge smile on his face, he looked up at the crowd.

"Ladies and gentlemen, thank you of your patience. The new owner of Kennaway Coopers is…"

There was a now-traditional gap, beloved of competition announcers as Richard Styles built up the tension.

Chapter Three

*And the twain were casting dice;
The game is done! I've won! I've won!'
Quoth she, and whistles thrice.*

"The new owner is… Ella Raleigh of Otterbury!"

There was a spontaneous gasp from the crowd dotted around the garden. Everyone looked around at everyone else. Those nearest to Ella turned towards her with delighted expressions on their faces. It was almost as if they had won themselves. Ella stood there bemused but with a broad smile on her face.

"I think that's you," whispered Frank.

"I think you're right. I didn't expect that!" Ella turned to Frank and hugged him.

Richard Styles' voice boomed out: "Ella Raleigh of Otterbury? Are you with us today?"

Ella tentatively raised her hand with her face buried in Frank's chest.

"Ah, I see a hand raised, over there, by the yew trees."

The whole crowd turned, as one, to see who it was.

"Come on down, Ella, and claim your prize!"

Ella walked slowly through the crowd towards the front steps. Frank followed at a respectable distance. People started applauding and shouting out cries of congratulations.

"Well done!"

"Make sure you keep it local!"

"Yeah, local jobs for local workers."

"You're not related, are you?"

Ella smiled and shook her head.

"Good old Otterbury!"

Ella reached the front steps. Richard Styles moved towards her and shook her hand.

"How does it feel to be the new owner of Kennaway Coopers?"

Ella smiled and said nothing.

"Right, overwhelmed by the occasion. Come with me, Ella and let's open the barrel."

Richard Giles led her over to Alice Aylesbeare who was stood waiting by the table.

Alice quietly congratulated her, out of range of the microphone. "Well done, Ella. Fancy meeting you here!"

Once again Ella smiled.

Richard Styles took an envelope out of his pocket, opened and handed Ella a shiny brass key, about three inches in length. He then took Ella's hand with the key in it and held it up high.

"Here's the key, ladies and gentlemen."

He shuffled Ella over to the barrel on the table. Alice came forward and lifted up the barrel to make it easier for Ella to insert the key.

"Just put the key in the lock, turn it and open the door."

Ella did exactly as Richard Styles said.

The key turned smoothly in the lock, the door swung open and Ella peered inside. She pulled out another envelope and having checked that there was nothing else in the barrel, moved away.

Ella, no longer smiling, turned towards Alice.

"Are you OK, Ella?"

"This is getting too much. I don't like standing up here in front of everyone and being gawped at! I think I'd like to open this with my husband and out of the eyes of the general public, please."

"No problem, leave it to me."

Alice went across to Richard Styles. She spoke to him, making sure that the microphone picked up her words.

"Richard, I don't think Ella is feeling too well. She says the occasion is getting the better of her. Why don't you wrap up the presentation and I'll find Ella a quieter place to calm down and relax?"

Richard Styles, ever the professional, turned towards those still remaining in the front gardens of Kennaway Court.

"Well, ladies and gentlemen, that appears to be that for the afternoon. The new owner of Kennaway Coopers is going into Kennaway Court to discuss arrangements with Caleb Kennaway and the rest of the family. So, all that remains to be said is thank you for your attendance, have a safe journey home and don't forget to tell your friends and family to listen to Richard "Miles of Smiles" Styles, every afternoon, on Radio East Devon. Now, it's back to the studio for the latest news and traffic updates. How's that mangel-wurzel spillage in Axminster? Is the road clear yet?"

~~

Alice and Ella were approached by Caleb. "Would you like to come into the house, Mrs…"

"Raleigh, Ella Raleigh."

"Yes, Mrs Raleigh. Is your husband around?"

"Yes, at the bottom of the steps. Frank?"

Ella, Frank and Alice followed Caleb through the front door and into Kennaway Court.

The reception hall was oak floored. There were large mirrors placed at regular intervals around the oak-panelled hallway. It gave the whole area an effect of light and space even though the only windows were halfway up the sumptuous stone stairway that led to the upper floors. The windows were arched with stone supports. The carved oak bannister had a newel post in the shape of an otter. The stairway was partly covered with expensive-looking patterned carpet. At the top of the staircase was an oak bannister balcony.

Ella looked around her with awe, taking in the whole experience. If the entrance area was meant to impress a visitor, then, in Ella's opinion, it had certainly succeeded.

"Please, come through to the drawing-room." Caleb shepherded the three of them through the entrance hall and into another majestic room. Ella looked around, once again, in awe. The room looked out through a large bay window onto a garden that was more like a park. There was half height oak panelling all around the room. Ella looked up at the ceiling which appeared to be hand-painted. She could pick out gold leaf motifs and intricately painted plasterwork.

Ella found herself speaking to Caleb "What a beautiful room. What lovely gardens. What an incredible house!"

Frank nodded in agreement but remained silent.

"Thank you, we bought it about twelve years ago. The company was making too much profit, so we decided to invest that profit in bricks and mortar."

"It's a bit more than bricks and mortar."

"Well, yes, it's scrubbed up nicely."

Caleb sat them all down around a large oak table.

"I gather you wanted to open the envelope away from the hubbub of Richard Styles and the good people of Ottery?"

"Yes, please. I'd like to discuss this all with my husband. Alone."

Caleb looked disappointed. "Are you sure?"

"Yes. I'd like to share this moment with my husband."

Caleb smiled and started to get up from his chair.

"Not a problem. Mrs Aylesbeare and I will leave you in peace. See that bell over the fireplace?"

Ella turned around and located the object.

"Just ring it if you need any assistance."

"I will. Oh, and Alice can stay if you don't mind? Mrs Aylesbeare and I are friends. We met in Budleigh Salterton. I'd value her opinion."

"Right you are, then. I'll see you in a while." Caleb left them with a smile of anticipation as he closed the oak door behind him.

Frank and Ella breathed a sigh of relief.

"Well, I didn't expect today to turn out like this," Ella whispered.

Frank smiled and Ella held out the envelope to him. "You open it."

Frank took it and looked around. On an antique oak school–desk by the window was a letter opener. He went over to the desk, picked it up and returned.

"Might as well do this properly!"

He sliced open the sealed edge and took out a couple of pieces of paper.

The first piece was an official-looking letter. Frank passed it to Ella. "No, you read it. I'll just sit here and listen."

"If you're certain?"

"Yes."

Frank read: *"To the winner of the Ottery Lottery. Congratulations. Before you take control of my company, I'd like to make certain that you're prepared for the task."*

"I thought there would be a catch!" Ella sighed.

Frank read on: *"The deeds to the company are buried in a miniature beer barrel. It is the same design as the one that contained this letter. It is buried within the boundaries of Ottery St Mary. Your task will be to follow my clues and claim it. Then the company is yours. However…"*

"Here comes another catch!"

"…the barrel must be found before Tar Barrel Night otherwise I am donating the whole of the company and its assets to my wife's charity in Albania."

"I bet the clues are so difficult that we'll never find the barrel." Ella was not feeling too positive.

"It goes on." Frank continued reading.

"None of the clues are too difficult and I sincerely hope you solve them all before Tar Barrel Night. You have plenty of time. The first clue is to be found on the other piece of paper in the envelope. Good luck. Yours very sincerely, Caleb Kennaway."

Ella took the letter from Frank's hands and re-read its contents. "Do we really want to go through all this hassle to own this company? Then when we get the company, if we get the company…"

"There'll be more hassle?"

"Exactly."

"And to think we moved down here to East Devon for the quiet life," Frank groaned.

"Well, at least, it's not a murder occupying our thoughts this time."

Alice smiled at both of them and said: "I suppose, at your age, it's all a bit too much of a challenge."

Frank and Ella both turned towards her. Alice had a look of sympathetic understanding on her face. At least, that's what Frank thought it was. After a few silent seconds, both Ella and Alice burst out laughing.

"Too much of a challenge. Fiddlesticks. Pass me the other piece of paper, please, Frank!"

The paper was light green in colour with flowery decorated scalloped edges. Ella opened the folded sheet of paper. On it were two lines of cryptic poetry.

"A safe repose, the seeker looks where once a bank, now houses books."

"Oh, a riddle," chuckled Alice. "I love riddles."

"There's something else in the envelope," said Ella, "It's a key."

"Another brass key?" asked Alice.

"No, looks like a key to one of those boxes you keep your precious keepsakes in!"

"It's time we spoke to Mr Kennaway again," said Frank.

"Could you ring the bell, Alice?" asked Ella.

"Oh, yes, please. It's like being in Downton Abbey!"

She pressed the button buzzer by the fireplace. They could all hear it ringing somewhere in the distance. After a wait of about thirty seconds, there was a knock on the door and in walked Caleb Kennaway. "You rang, sir and madams?"

"Yes, we've read your letter and your riddle," replied Ella. "Both Frank and I are willing to play along with this little game."

"Just one thing before we agree." Frank interrupted.

"Yes, fire away!"

"There actually *are* deeds to the company when we solve this clue?"

"No," said Caleb, "there are several clues. At the end of those clues, there is a miniature beer barrel and it does contain the deeds. When you open the barrel and remove the deeds, they and Kennaway Coopers belong to you."

Ella looked at him with a thoughtful expression on her face. "Why are you doing this, Mr Kennaway?"

"Running this company is addictive. For all these years, I've loved every minute. But I've got to break this addiction and find out if there's more to life than work. I don't need the money. I want to find out if I need the hassle anymore."

"And if you do need the hassle, are you going to want the company back?" asked Ella.

"Oh no. I've made my mind up. I'm going to retire and enjoy this house for the rest of my life. I have more than enough money to last me to my grave, even beyond. I want to build up a bank of memories with my family and friends."

He looked at both Frank and Ella. "You know, I think you're up to solving my little puzzles. When you've solved the first one, come back here and we'll discuss the running of the business. Now, there should be a key in the envelope. I'm going to look after it for you. When you need it, come and ask me and I'll willingly hand it over."

Ella passed the key to him.

"When will we need it?"

"Oh, you'll know, you'll know."

Caleb put the key in his pocket before resuming. "Maybe, I'll show you around the works and let you shadow some of my best and most valued workers. Give you a feel for the place."

Frank and Ella both nodded in agreement.

"I guarantee, once you've become used to the idea, you're going to love running the company. It'll be an addiction for you as well!"

Frank and Ella bid him farewell. Alice went off to find her colleague. "Good luck," she uttered. "If you want any help solving a riddle, give me a call."

"We will. See you soon, Alice."

Ella took hold of Frank's hand and they walked down the drive and off to find their car in Land of Canaan car park.

She murmured as they walked: *"A safe repose, the seeker looks where once a bank, now houses books."*

Chapter Four

Late, late yestreen I saw the new Moon,
With the old Moon in her arms;
And I fear, I fear, My Master dear!
We shall have a deadly storm.

That evening in the cool twilight of Kennaway Court's drawing-room, Caleb faced an angry board of directors as they tried to discuss the future of Kennaway Coopers.

"She didn't look as if she could manage a Sunday School tea party," grumbled Carl.

"Be fair, you've never even spoken to her, or her husband." Caleb was prepared for the backlash.

"I don't need to speak to the pair. They looked totally out of their depth."

"They're going to ruin all our hard work," added Carl.

"In a year's time, Kennaway Coopers will be bankrupt," Kenneth asserted.

"If I put you in charge, Kennaway Coopers would be bankrupt within the month, let alone a year!"

"There's no call for that. If you'd given me more responsibility, then you would have seen how capable I am."

"I know how capable you are. I still remember the Bideford deal."

"One error of judgement. And anyway, that was two years ago."

"And the Norton Cider arrangement. And Sowden Valley. To say nothing of my having to rescue you from the clutches of the Lyme cider lady." Caleb counted the incidents on his fingers.

"I'm learning from my mistakes!"

"Yes, with my money! Enough is enough."

Christine Kennaway stood between father and son.

"There's still time to change your mind. No-one would be surprised," announced Christine.

"Yes, owners do it all the time." Kenneth nodded.

"Let me offer you… oh, just name your price." Carl spoke up.

"I already have. The price is winning the Ottery Lottery."

"What about a million? Two million? Three million?"

"No, Carl, you're too late. You're all too late. I've made my mind up. It's my business and I'll do as I see fit."

"Fit? No, your decision proves you're unfit. Unfit to run the company and unfit to give it away like this." Christine wagged her finger in his direction. "Whoever's heard of someone giving away a company?"

"And a profitable one at that!" added Carl.

"You're mad!" spluttered Kenneth.

"Unfit. Mad. Out of control." Christine was getting angry.

"I've never been saner. Your words prove that to me. Not one of you has been even a little bit supportive of my motives."

"Because your motives are wrong," continued Christine. "An outsider wouldn't understand the business. It'd take a number of years."

"The expertise is here," explained Fabian. "In this room."

"Yes, you're right. My expertise. I've had to run this firm almost single-handedly in the last year. Christine's too busy with her charity. Kenneth's too busy making mistakes. Fabian wants to sell to Bavaria. Carl's too scared to take risks–too busy with his health and safety. I'm the only one who's kept this company moving forward. And now, I've had enough."

"Don't talk more rubbish," muttered Christine.

"I couldn't let any one of you take the reins of Kennaway Coopers. You'd run it into the ground at the first sign of trouble."

The argument continued in the same vein for another half an hour. At last, Caleb stood up, pushed his chair under the oak table and held up one hand.

"Enough! That seems like my favourite word at the moment!"

The room went silent.

"I'm heard enough this evening to convince me that I'm doing the right thing. I've had enough of your futile arguments. I've had enough of everything today to know I need a good night's sleep. So, if you'll excuse me, I'm heading off to bed. Don't make too much of a noise on your way out."

Caleb opened the drawing-room door and headed for the stairs. There was a clatter of chairs behind him as Christine, Kenneth, Fabian and Carl all got up and followed him.

"You can't just walk away like that?" cried Kenneth bringing his drink with him.

"What about the company?" asked Fabian.

"I think I've said enough for tonight. Enough. I'm not going to change my mind."

Caleb started to climb the stairs towards the bedrooms. The four fellow directors followed him. At the top of the stairs, the upper gallery was boarded by the oaken bannisters. Frank leaned on them and watched with a look of exasperated amusement on his face.

"Are you all coming to bed as well? I'm not sure my bed's big enough for the five of us!"

"Don't be facetious, Caleb." Christine was not happy.

"And don't run away," shouted Kenneth. "We're trying to talk some sense into you."

"Well, you're wasting your time. I already have all the senses I need. All five of them. I don't want to touch, see, hear, taste or smell any of you anymore tonight. That includes you, Christine. I'm going to sleep in one of the guest rooms."

Kenneth had moved beyond Caleb and barred his way. He took a gulp of his drink.

"Now, listen here, Daddy."

"Oh, it's Daddy now. It's always Daddy when you want money!"

"You never listen otherwise." Kenneth finished off the last of the alcohol in his glass.

"And I think you've had more than enough drink for tonight."

"That's not fair!"

The discussion lost whatever dignity it had possessed and descended into a slanging match. It went on and on, round and around in circles. Every time Caleb attempted to escape, someone barred his way. The decibel level continued to rise. It seemed an attempt was being made to wake up the whole town of Ottery St Mary.

Eventually, at the apex of some extremely rude accusations, Caleb pushed past Kenneth, almost ran down the corridor, into a guest room and locked the door behind him.

Mrs Kennaway hammered on the door and demanded her husband come out and face the music like a man. Caleb ignored her. One by one the directors, with a collective shrug of some angry shoulders, turned on their heels. They sidled off downstairs and made their way to their own places of rest.

Only Mrs Kennaway remained. She leaned against the door and screamed: "One of these days, someone is going to really lose their temper with you, Caleb Kennaway."

Kenneth shouted up from the foot of the stairs. "Yes, and it might well be me, father!"

"I hope you live to regret your stupid decision." Christine angrily turned and shuffled off alone to her bedroom.

"What are you doing up at this time of night?"

"More to the point, what are you?" Caleb answered.

They both stood facing each other on the landing.

"I couldn't sleep. So I thought I'd come and talk to you one more time."

"You're mad to think it'll do any good."

"Maybe, but I'm angry as well. You're ruining everything."

"Just go away. Leave me alone. I'm going downstairs to get a drink."

"A whisky won't make your stupid decision go away."

"I said just leave me alone." Caleb pushed out at his angry accuser.

"Don't you hit me!" The accuser pushed back forcefully towards the bannisters.

"What are you doing?"

"This!"

Once more Caleb was pushed backwards. His hip hit one of the bannister supports with his full force. It snapped and Caleb fell backwards into thin air.

"What?" Caleb's face had an expression of unbelieving surprise as he plummeted to the solid oak floor below.

꩜

The next morning Frank and Ella sat down in the front room with their marvellous view of Mutter's Moor and considered the riddle.

"*A safe repose, the seeker looks. Where once a bank, now houses books,*" Ella repeated. "We must be the seekers."

"True."

"What's a safe repose? A bed?"

"A shelter. Are there any bus shelters in Ottery?"

"You mean like the one in Staverton?" laughed Ella.

"Could be. The barrel could be buried underneath the bus shelter."

"I think not! We're getting into the realms of fantasy here, Corporal Jones!"

Frank saluted whilst Ella stared at the riddle once more. "Houses books? What houses books?"

"A bookshop?"

"A library?"

"Are there any bookshops in Ottery?" asked Frank.

"Yes, there is one, I think. And there's a newsagent. There's also a library."

"Where?"

"In the middle of town. Where the old NatWest used to be."

"Of course," cried Frank. "That's it! They have safes in a bank. The barrel will be in the safe."

"But the bank's now a library? Would a library have a safe?"

"They may have left one behind," enthused Frank. "Those old safes weighed a ton. Perhaps it was built into the building. The barrel could be buried behind it."

"Or in it! Is the library open today?"

Frank consulted his iPad. "Yes, from ten o'clock until one o'clock."

"What are we waiting for? Watch out deeds, we're coming to get you!"

Frank and Ella jumped in their car and sped to Ottery St Mary. They parked in the superstore car-park and made their way to the library.

A lovely old lady librarian stood by her desk helping two dear ladies looking for the latest Agatha Raisin. Frank and Ella waited behind the librarian. She found the book they were looking for and then had to referee a loud discussion about who should read it first.

When they had finished, Frank quietly whispered: "Excuse me, can you help? We're looking for a safe?" The old lady didn't react, so he tapped her on the shoulder and repeated the question.

"Hello," she said. "You'll have to speak up. My batteries are running out."

"I think she means her hearing aid," giggled Ella.

For the third time, Frank repeated his question. This time in a louder voice. A gentleman reading a newspaper nearby turned around and shushed Frank.

"Don't mind George, he'd be asleep if it got too quiet!"

"Have you got a safe in this building?" asked Frank.

"A safe? We're a library, not a bank."

"But this building used to be a bank, didn't it?" added Ella.

"Yes, you're correct. You know, I do think we have an old safe. In the back room. The bank left it behind when they vacated the building. It's not very big and it's broken. The door doesn't lock properly. A safe's not much good if the door won't close!" She laughed at the absurdity of it and was met with another shush from George.

"Can we see the safe, please?" asked Ella.

"I suppose so. Can't think of a reason why not. It won't have anything in it."

She led them through a door into the back room. There were trolleys of library books parked along one wall and a small dusty black metal safe underneath the only window in the room. The safe door was slightly open and, leaning down, both Frank and Ella could see a piece of paper lying there on its own within the safe.

"The deeds?" queried Frank.

Ella reached in and picked the paper up. It looked exactly the same as the riddle paper. Light green paper folded in half with flowery decorated scalloped edges.

"Not another riddle?" sighed Frank.

"I'm afraid so. It's definitely not the deeds!"

Ella was correct. She unfolded the sheet and read its contents aloud:

"A tower to train for times of heat, Look underneath the highest seat."

"Another cryptic clue!"

"Well, we've solved one clue. We can solve another."

"How many clues are there going to be?"

"Caleb Kennaway said he'd talk to us again when we'd solved the first clue. Well, we have, so let's go and speak to the man."

Frank turned to thank the lady librarian, but she had left the room and was tapping George on the shoulder. "Have you gone to sleep again?"

Frank and Ella quietly meandered back through the library and out into the street. They trudged up the hill and made their way past the church down College Lane to Kennaway Court. As they walked through the open gates, they were greeted with the sight of a police car parked across the drive. Leaning against the passenger door was PC Alf Hydon.

"Hello, what are you doing here, Alf?" said Ella.

"Has there been a burglary or something?" asked Frank.

PC Hydon stood up properly and faced them. "No, far worse than that. Somebody be dead."

"Oh no!" uttered Ella. "Well, we were coming here to speak to Caleb Kennaway. Perhaps, it'll be better if we came back another day."

"We could always phone and make an appointment," mused Frank.

"Won't do you no good."

"Why ever not?"

"They found a dead person at the foot of the main stairs in Kennaway Court this morning. Caleb Kennaway."

Chapter Five

*With many a pause and oft reverted eye
I climb the Coomb's ascent*

"Dead? Caleb Kennaway? But we spoke to him only yesterday."

"Was it a heart attack?"

"Was the pressure of yesterday all too much for him?"

"I can't comment," replied PC Hydon. He stood away from the car and placed his police hat firmly on his head. "You can ask the Sergeant. Here she comes now."

Sergeant Knowle smiled as she approached the car. "I wondered how long it would be before you two turned up!"

"We've come to see Caleb," explained Ella.

"I presume PC Hydon has told you what's happened."

"Yes, Caleb's dead. How sad." Ella was genuine in her sadness. "I liked him. He seemed to know what he wanted out of his life."

"Well, not anymore."

"How did he die?" Frank asked.

"Well, as far as we can tell, he may have either fallen down the stairs or he could have crashed through the bannisters. The housekeeper found him this morning. He cracked his head on the floor. At least, we assume it was the floor. It could have been the bannister or the stairs."

"Or somebody hit him?"

"That, of course, is another line of enquiry!"

"Typical," Frank muttered, "we come down to East Devon for the easy life, a bit of peace and quiet and we've already become mixed up in two murders. I just pray that this is not a third one!"

"Let's not get ahead of ourselves," Sergeant Knowle warned. "The forensic team is doing its work later today once they finish up a suspicious death in Pinhoe. The family and staff have been confined to a couple of rooms at the back of the house."

"So, you think it may be a suspicious death?" queried Ella.

"I really don't know until we forensics have done their job!"

"We'll have to employ thee again," chortled PC Hydon.

"Yes, I'll see the ACC if it is murder. You're doing well at the moment–two out of two! But let's hope you're not needed."

The four of them stood around for a bit talking about nothing much in particular.

Sergeant Knowle broke into the tittle–tattle. "Wait a minute, I forgot to ask you about your new acquisition."

Ella looked a little confused.

"Kennaway Coopers!"

"Oh yes, that's why we're here. It's all a bit strange." Ella explained about the clues and that the deeds were buried in a barrel somewhere in Ottery St Mary.

"I think you'd better give the family a ring later in the week," Sergeant Knowle suggested. "If it is murder, I'll contact you. You could be most helpful. After all, you'll be able to see the family and the company workers as part of your legitimate business. You'll be our spies on the inside!"

Frank and Ella went back into the middle of Ottery and found a coffee shop in Silver Street. It looked like a lovely old fashioned tea room. The coffee was good. There were no modern-day distractions. Even though the place was well populated, the atmosphere was respectfully peaceful. The elderly customers appeared to be locals. It was no surprise to hear that the news about Caleb's death had spread like wildfire through the town. Everyone in the shop was quietly gossiping about it. Fortunately, no-one recognised them from yesterday, so Frank and Ella found a quiet corner away from the main areas of discussion and, keeping their heads down, tried to solve the second clue.

Frank read out the clue. "*A tower to train for times of heat, Look underneath the highest seat.*"

"What are the important words and what do they mean?" Ella asked.

"Tower, train, times of heat, highest seat."

"A tower could be a church tower or a tall building. Is there a castle in Ottery?"

"Not that I know about. A train? Could be a train station?"

"Didn't there used to be a train station on the other side of the river?"

"Yes, I remember reading about it somewhere. It was on the Sidmouth branch line. The railway went from Sidmouth Junction, up near Feniton, through Ottery, Otterbury and Tipton and on to Sidmouth."

"Is there a water tower at the old station? Perhaps the water was needed to cool down the trains in times of heat."

"Maybe there's a chair, or seat, on or beside the water tower?"

"The deeds may be buried underneath the seat!"

"Let's take a walk down there after we finish our coffee."

"Hold on. Relax. We need to take our time. We've been rushing about like a pair of teenagers for the past couple of days. Let's enjoy these drinks and try to listen to the gossip."

※

Forty-five minutes later Frank and Ella made their way down Mill Street, past the new houses. "Lovely houses but I hope they've got good drainage!" mused Frank. "If the Otter floods they could be in trouble."

"I'm sure they've thought about that. People don't build houses these days without taking those sorts of things into account."

Frank dismissed a touch of cynicism by keeping silent. They moved on, across St Saviour's Bridge and into the industrial estate.

"Right, we're looking for a water tower on the site of the old station."

They quickly found the old station. Someone had helpfully named the building, The Station. It was a community centre. As they made their way towards it, a middle-aged lady came out of the front doors.

"Hello," greeted Ella, "Can you help us?"

"I'll try, me dear."

"We're looking for the water tower at the old station."

"Well, this be the old station but it never 'ad a warter tower."

"Are you sure," said Frank.

"Absolutely certain. There be no towers round 'ere at all."

"Well, thanks. Sorry to disturb you."

"That's alright, me dears." The lady scratched her chin and then offered some more information. "Have you tried the fire station?"

"No. Why?"

"They got a tower. Gurt big metal thing. They use it for training. It's near the supermarket."

Ella shouted, "Yes, of course!"

Frank grasped the lady's right hand and shook it very firmly. "Thank you, thank you, thank you! You've been so helpful!"

"Glad to be of service."

She stood there, hands on hips, as Frank and Ella scooted away back towards the bridge.

"*A tower to train for times of heat.* Fireman fight fires, fires are hot. The tower is used for training. It's so obvious, really!"

"Why didn't we think of it?"

"I suppose we needed to think outside of the box."

"I bet this tower has got a seat at the top."

They made their back along Mill Street, turned into Canaan Way and found the fire station opposite the Medical centre. "Is this place still open? They've closed a lot of fire stations in the last few years."

Fortunately, it was still open, and they found one of the firemen outside the main building maintaining the fire engine.

"Excuse me, can you help us?" Frank asked.

"That's my job. Station Master Harry Abbott at your service. Have you got a fire that needs putting out?"

"No. We're looking for a beer barrel."

"A miniature one," explained Ella.

"You could try one of the gift shops in the town centre. We don't drink beer on duty."

"No, we're not making ourselves very clear," said Ella.

"A friend of ours set us a riddle. He told us that a beer barrel would be found under a seat at the top of your fire training tower."

"Oh, so you're the treasure seekers."

"I suppose so." Frank wasn't sure if he was being serious.

"Yes, Caleb, from the Coopers. He came along a few weeks ago and told us all about his little game."

"So, there is a seat at the top of the tower?" asked Ella.

"There certainly is. It's one of my deck chairs from my garden shed."

"Can we go up there and look underneath it?"

"No and yes."

"What do you…"

"You, sir, can go up there but you, madam can't."

"That's discrimination," protested Ella.

"No, madame, it's height. You're not tall enough to be allowed up there. We have to have a cut-off point. Just like at the amusement parks. However, climbing towers is no game."

"I understand. I don't agree, but I understand," commented Ella.

"Well, lead the way," said Frank, "Where's the first ladder?"

"Wait a minute, sir. You can't just climb up a tower without being prepared. Let's have a look at your shoes."

The Station Master peered at Frank's footwear and tut-tutted. "That won't do." His gaze then took in Frank's trousers, a pair of casual slim fit chinos. He repeated his "Tut-tut!"

Frank's jacket elicited the same reaction. "You'll need to be kitted up properly. You come with me. We'll find something suitable for climbing towers."

Frank shrugged his shoulders and followed Station Master Abbott. Ella stood there, not knowing whether to be angry or dissolve into fits of giggles.

Ten minutes later, Frank re-appeared wearing a strong pair of fireman boots, some hard-wearing trousers and a yellow-edged fireman jacket. Station Master Abbott was dressed in a similar fashion with the addition of a smart yellow helmet. He was also carrying another helmet under his arm.

"Frank, why aren't you wearing your helmet?" called Ella.

"Madam, we couldn't find a helmet for his size of head. We found a couple too small for him and another way too large. Now, he couldn't wear that helmet climbing these ladders. It could slip over his eyes and he'd be a goner."

"Why have you got that helmet under your arm, then?"

"Yes, that's your helmet. Regulations dictate that visitors who may be in the vicinity of high risk activities may be asked to wear helmets. I'm asking you to wear a helmet. Please put it on."

Ella laughed. "I can't wear that! It'll just sit there on the end of my nose. I won't be able to see a thing!"

"That's the idea, madame. You don't want to see if something goes wrong."

"What? No, wait a minute. Frank needs a helmet."

"Don't worry. He's my responsibility."

"But…"

"No buts. Put the helmet on."

Ella complied. Under protest.

"Now, your husband has signed a disclaimer. He tells me his personal accident insurance is up to date, so let's go."

Frank and Harry made their way to the foot of the tower. The tower was made up of five floors. There was a ladder leading up from one floor to the next. Each floor looked like a metal grid. The whole structure was open-sided and made of latticed steelwork. There was even a radio mast on the top and what looked like a television aerial on the far side.

Ella held the helmet up so she could see. It looked very dangerous. She fully expected Stationmaster Abbott to call time on the exercise. But to her dismay, Frank and Harry started to climb to the first floor. Frank led the way and Harry followed behind. "Ready to catch him if he falls," thought Ella.

At the first floor, Harry shook Frank by the hand and took out a safety harness on some sort and fastened him to the ladder. Frank climbed to the second floor yet again followed by Harry. Once more, Harry shook Frank's hand. This time Frank turned around and spied Ella below holding up her helmet. He gave her the thumbs up and stood there as Harry ascended the next two ladders to the top. He shouted to Frank, "There's no beer barrel only this plastic envelope."

"Are you sure?"

"Come on up if you don't believe me!"

"No, thank you. I'm as high as I'm going to climb."

"Fair enough. I'll bring it down with me." He tucked the envelope into a large zipped pocket in his jacket and descended back to Frank.

"This time, I'll lead the way. Feel for each step with your leading foot and get a good grip before you move. Make sure your heel is up against the rung. You shouldn't have to look down at all. We'll keep the safety harness on until you reach the ground now."

Frank felt his way slowly down the rungs, feeling more confident as each step brought him closer to terra firma. Harry unclipped and re-clipped the harness to the last ladder and they made their way successfully to the ground.

Ella clapped and went to hug him as Frank left the last rung. "Well done. My hero. You made it up two levels."

"Yes," interrupted Harry, "that's more than most people do. Your husband did well. I never expected him to get up any of the floors. I was just teasing you, but he proved me wrong. If he were a few years younger, then he'd have a wonderful career in the Fire Service."

"I've never been so scared, since… I don't know when!" gulped Frank.

"There wasn't a miniature beer barrel up there, was there?" asked Ella.

"No. Only this envelope wrapped in plastic to keep out the rain. I put it up there for Caleb Kennaway a few weeks ago. It's all yours."

"Then you knew all about this?"

"Yep! I told you I knew about his little game."

"You could have gone up there for us?"

"Yep!"

"Frank needn't have had to get all dressed up?"

"Nope!"

"I needn't have worn this helmet!"

"Nope!"

"Well…" Ella had run out of words.

"Think of it as an initiation. A rite of passage. And think about all the fun you had! And the tales you can tell your children and grandchildren!"

"I think we've had our share of tales to tell in the past few months. We moved to East Devon for a quiet life."

"No chance of that down 'ere. This is where the action is… not in the big city but here in the countryside."

"I'm beginning to think you're right. Can I have the envelope now?"

Stationmaster Harry Abbott took out the envelope from his jacket pocket and handed it to Ella. She opened the plastic clip and drew out another envelope. She ripped it open and pulled out a piece of light green paper folded in half with flowery decorated scalloped edges.

"It's another clue, isn't it," sighed Frank.

Ella read out the writing on the paper.

> *"Go cross the bridge, I bid you well,*
> *To find a lot of mine won't sell."*

Chapter Six

*To meet, to know, to love–and then to part,
Is the sad tale of many a human heart.*

"Another clue! How many do we have to solve?" Frank had exchanged his fireman uniform for his everyday clothes. They had thanked Harry Abbott for his help.

Frank grudgingly admitted, "It was an experience that I enjoyed, I think. Although I'm not sure if I'd want to do it again."

"Next time we'll take you to the top. It's a grand view!"

🙦🙤

They sat in their car staring at the third piece of green scalloped paper.

"Let's go home and sit down with a cup of tea. Maybe liquid refreshment will help our brains solve this riddle!"

As they sat down ready to do battle with another clue, the phone rang. Frank said "Hello?" and was pleased to hear the voice of Sergeant Knowle.

"Hi, Frank. Just thought you'd like to know the latest on Caleb Kennaway."

"Certainly. Yes, please. Just let me put you on speaker–phone so that Ella can hear as well."

"Not a problem. Hiya, Ella!"

"Hiya Elsie! What's the news?"

"Well, Caleb Kennaway died from a blow to the head. There are two options our wizards are following. Either he was hit at the top of the stairs. If he was, then that points to murder. If he hit his head when he landed, then that could just be a tragic accident."

"I recall a while ago that you thought another death was a tragic accident, didn't you?"

"Yes, but you proved me wrong about that. So, I'm keeping an open mind on this one!"

"Could he have just fallen down the stairs?"

"You haven't been to the scene of the crime, have you? The bannister above where his body was found was snapped. It was made of oak. It must have taken an almighty shove to push him through it."

"That sounds like intent to murder!"

"Looks like it!"

"Who might be our suspects?" Frank asked.

"Well, at least four people were seen and heard having the dickens of an argument on the evening before. His wife, his son and two company directors."

"What was the argument about?"

"Have a guess?"

"Kennaway Coopers? The fact that he's given away the company?"

"Exactly. Spot on!"

"Their fingerprints are all the bannisters and I bet, they'll be all over his clothing as well. We're waiting for the DNA results."

"How can we help?"

"Well, you're involved already. As the new boss of Kennaway Coopers, you'll need to be talking to all four of them. Talk to them. Question them, in a non-threatening manner, of course. Find out what you can. But…., and I can't stress this enough, stay safe!"

"Oh, don't worry about that. We've learned our lessons!"

"Have you? I'm not so sure. Just take care."

"Can we go and see any of them yet?"

"You certainly can. I've asked to interview all of them the day after tomorrow. I want to interview you two as well. Carl Cooper, one of the directors told me that it seemed a bit of a coincidence that Caleb died just after he'd given the company away to you."

"That's ridiculous. We wouldn't want to kill him."

"No, you know that, and I know that. But let's keep it all as a level playing field."

"Which police station are you meeting at?" Frank inquired.

"None. We've been invited to Kennaway Court. I thought we'd keep the conversations as pleasant and low key as possible, so I accepted their invitation. Ten thirty in the morning, the day after tomorrow. Be there, or I'll have to issue a warrant for your arrest."

"There's no need to go that far. We'll be there."

೩∞

This time there was no police car in the drive as Frank and Ella walked up to the front door.

"Ten thirty on the dot," said Ella with a knowing smile.

They pulled a well-worn antique metal bell cord and the door was opened by Mrs Kennaway.

"Oh, it's you. Come in. The police aren't here yet."

They followed her into the drawing-room. There were three gentlemen already sat around the large oak table.

"Have a seat. I'll ring for some coffee."

Mrs. Kennaway sat down and pointed to her right. "This is my son, Kenneth." He nodded in greeting.

"Over there by the window is Carl Cooper and this gentleman is Fabian Fassbender. They are, or were, directors of the company."

"Still are! Until we see the deeds," muttered Kenneth.

"Quite," Carl Cooper added. "And who are you?"

"My name is Ella Raleigh, and this is my husband Frank. My ticket was picked out the other day. I won the Ottery Lottery. I will be the new owner of Kennaway Coopers."

"How much do you want?" asked Mrs. Kennaway.

"How much are you offering?" countered Frank.

The answer never came as the front door bell rang again and Mrs. Kennaway stood up, looked at the ceiling in frustration, and scuttled out of the room. Thirty seconds of uncomfortable silence passed until the heavy footsteps of PC Hydon heralded his entrance into the room.

"Morning all," he announced, taking off his helmet and smoothing down his hair.

Sergeant Knowle and Mrs. Kennaway followed him into the room. Sergeant Knowle took control of the situation straightaway. "Good morning, everyone, thank you for gathering here. I'm sure introductions have been made. I'm Sergeant Knowle and this is my colleague, PC Hydon."

She smiled but, apart from Ella, no-one smiled back.

"This morning I'd like to interview each of you separately about the events of the other day with particular emphasis on the evening discussions. We've already interviewed the three members of staff. The cook heard the very loud discussion on her way out and the other two had already left the building earlier in the evening. All three of them have alibis for the rest of the evening and all through the night. I am completely satisfied that they are not involved in the unfortunate death of Caleb Kennaway."

Sergeant Knowle paused for breath. Carl Cooper raised his right hand. "Sergeant, how did poor Caleb die? I assumed he fell down the stairs, but I've just seen, on my way in, the broken bannister."

"Thank you, Mr. Cooper. As you can probably guess by this meeting, we are not satisfied with the manner of his death. We are leaning towards the conclusion that Caleb Kennaway may have been murdered."

Sergeant Knowle and PC Hydon led Carl Cooper out of the room leaving the others to ponder upon the revelation.

"Murdered," drawled Kenneth. "Who killed him? And how?"

"I thought he fell," said Fabian. He looked across at Mrs. Kennaway. "You said he fell."

"I thought that myself. He'd been drinking all evening."

"Were those bannisters particularly brittle?" ventured Ella.

"Brittle! They were made of oak," scoffed Kenneth.

"Perhaps he took a running jump at them?" laughed Fabian.

"I don't think that's funny, Fabian." Kenneth gazed across–eyes like daggers.

"Sorry, just my German sense of humour."

"What about your discussion?" Frank asked, "Sergeant Knowle is bound to ask what it was all about."

"We were trying to persuade him to change his mind and not give away the company to your wife." Kenneth again jumped in to answer the question.

"Did the discussion become violent?"

"Not physically. We shouted a bit. We were all in here. He got fed up with us and went upstairs to bed. We followed him."

"Kenneth, dear, you sound as if you're rehearsing your answers for the police," interrupted Mrs. Kennaway.

"Mum, I'm telling the truth. I'll tell those two policemen the same thing."

☙❧

"Now, Mr. Cooper. Where were you between 10 pm and 11.30 pm on the night of Mr Kennaway's death?" Sergeant Knowle stared directly at Carl as she asked the question.

"Why do you need to know?"

"To eliminate you from this murder inquiry."

"I didn't kill the man. I needed him alive!"

"Mr. Cooper, where were you between 10 pm and 11.30 pm on the night of Mr Kennaway's death?" Sergeant Knowle repeated.

"Well, I was here at the house until about 9 o'clock and then I went to another meeting."

"And how long were you at this other meeting?"

"It finished at about 10.30. We were all at the London Inn. It wasn't a busy evening but quite a few people would have seen me arrive and depart."

"What was the meeting about?"

"Health and Safety. The alarming lack of health and safety in this town."

"And where did you go after the meeting?"

"Home. I arrived home at about 11 o'clock. Then I went to bed."

"And can anyone confirm this? Your wife? your partner?"

"My wife and I are separated at present. She has gone to live elsewhere."

"So no-one can confirm your whereabouts after 10.30 pm that evening?"

"No, I suppose not."

"Thank you, Mr. Cooper, that's all for now."

☙❧

The door opened and Carl Cooper slouched in. He looked tired and nervous. He sat down in an armchair in the corner of the room.

"Well?" Mrs. Kennaway said.

"No. Not really. They think one of us killed him."

"Preposterous. We've all got an alibi–except these two." She nodded her head towards Frank and Ella.

Frank nodded back and smiled.

PC Hydon appeared at the door. "Mr. Fassbender, please."

Fabian got up and followed the oversized policeman.

Kenneth stood up and strolled around the table towards Frank and Ella.

"What about you two? Have you got an alibi?"

"No, we're just like the rest of you. Our only alibi is each other." Frank again smiled and tried not to appear too smug or confident.

"Perhaps you came along after our little discussion broke up. Fabian and Carl left the house. I went up to my room on the other side of the house. Mum went to bed alone. Perhaps you phoned Caleb for a late-night discussion? Perhaps Caleb let you in? Did you try to get more than just the company? Did you want the house as well? Did he refuse and you got into an argument? Perhaps you chased him up the stairs and pushed him through the bannisters to the floor below?"

Kenneth stood there, astonished at his outburst.

"Perhaps," Frank replied, "but it sounds to me as if you're clutching at some very thin straws."

"I think that you're talking complete and utter rubbish," said Ella in a quiet controlled voice.

"Maybe," Kenneth added, "you're trying to deflect the questions away from you because…." He stopped and waved a hand in the air as if completing the sentence in some form of sign language.

"Kenneth, sit down. You're making a fool of yourself." The voice was louder than Ella's but just as authoritative. Kenneth obeyed his mother and lumbered back around the table and sat down.

There was a quiet reticence within the room. Frank wished he'd remembered to switch on the audio recorder on his phone. He just hoped he could reminder all the nuances of the conversations.

❧

"Now Mr. Fassbender. I'm sure that you're aware that a serious crime may have been committed the other evening?"

"People are saying it was murder?"

"They may be correct. So I need to ask you a few questions and I expect full answers. Do you understand?"

"Of course, I understand. You'll want to know where I was after our little argument?"

"Yes. And?"

"I left when Caleb went to bed. It seemed a waste of time to stick around. I drove home. I went up to Ladymount, crossed the A30, drove through Cranbrook and back to my flat. I live alone. Cranbrook is full of cameras. I'm sure one of them will have picked up my Mercedes."

"We'll check the cameras, obviously."

"I'll leave you my registration and car details."

"No need, Mr. Fassbender. We already have them. What's to say you didn't return to Kennaway Court later on?"

"I could have done, I suppose. But I didn't. You'll need to check your cameras."

"Thank you, Mr. Fassbender. That'll be all for now. We may need to question you again later. Perhaps when we've scoured the camera footage for our Mercedes!"

ೊೋ

Fabian soon arrived back in the room. He too went to sit in an armchair. He was silent and thoughtful. PC Hydon looked at Frank and beckoned him with his first finger.

Sergeant Knowle was waiting for him in a small room near the kitchen. The window looked out onto the drive.

"I wondered at first, if they'd all done for him," began the Sergeant.

"No, I don't think so," responded Frank. "I think he fell after their arguments. Someone came back to pick up the threads of the discussion again and when they discovered they were still getting nowhere, they got violent."

"Well, Carl said he went off to another meeting. Fabian told us he drove home. We'll need to check that."

"They both could have returned later and killed him."

"Absolutely." Sergeant Knowle sat there, staring out of the window. "I'm going to speak to Mrs. Kennaway next."

"No, I think you should speak to Kenneth. He's a bit of a loose cannon. He may tell you more. Mrs. Kennaway is too calm. Make her wait a little longer."

"OK. Alf, take Frank back and bring me Mister Kenneth Kennaway."

꒰ঌ

"Mr. Kennaway. Sorry to keep you waiting but we're going as quickly as we can. It's just a few questions. I'm sure we'll be back to ask you some more in the near future. But, for now, we'd like to know your movements after your discussion finished."

"Discussion? It was a full-blown argument. I'm surprised none of our neighbours reported it to you."

"What was it about?"

"The future of the company. After Dad gave it away to that lady back there." He jerked his thumb in the direction of the drawing-room.

"I assume you tried to make him change his mind?"

"Of course, we did. But he can be so stubborn sometimes. He felt we needed a breath of fresh air. I could understand that if he decided to bring in somebody who understood the business. But to give it away to a nobody."

"That's a bit harsh."

"Maybe, but it's true. We don't know who she is and what experience she's got. We tried to get Dad to change his mind and let Mum and me run the company, but he wouldn't budge."

"How did the evening end?"

"Well, to be honest, I'd had a bit too much to drink and I can't remember. Fabian told me that he dragged me along the corridor to my bedroom. I do know that I woke up in the morning in the same clothes I'd worn the day before and with a stinker of a headache."

"Fabian's Mr. Fassbender, yes?"

"Yes. Someone must have dumped me on the bed before they left."

"So for the rest of the night, you heard nothing?"

"No."

"And saw nothing?"

"Obviously not!"

"Could you have gone back to Mr. Kennaway's room in a drunken stupor and continued the argument?"

"I really don't know. I don't think so. But it has crossed my mind that I might have continued the argument. But I really can't remember! I could have been the one who pushed him through the bannisters. I could be his murderer!"

Chapter Seven

*In Xanadu did Kubla Khan
A stately pleasure-dome decree:
Where Alph, the sacred river, ran
Through caverns measureless to man
Down to a sunless sea.*

"Mrs Kennaway corroborated everybody else's story. Yes, Kenneth was drunk. Yes, Carl Cooper went on to a meeting. Yes, Fabian left as well. She didn't mention whether Fabian had helped Kenneth to bed. She only said that Kenneth went downstairs to get another drink."

Sergeant Elsie Knowle was sat in the Raleigh's front room with the view of Mutter's Moor facing her through the large window. PC Alf Hydon was away quelling a disagreement between two women on Sidmouth seafront.

Ella and Frank were intrigued to hear the contents of the interviews.

"We've taken DNA from each of the suspects and we'll see if their DNA appears on the clothes and body of Caleb. We're going to have to just wait for the results!"

"What do you want us to do?"

"You need to make some appearances at Kennaway Coopers. Be seen around the place. Get invited into the business premises and see if the employees can give us any more snippets of information. See if you can get into the good books of Kenneth and Christine

Kennaway. I'll check out Fabian Fassbender and the traffic cameras and I'll also check on Carl Cooper's alibi at his meeting."

"I know this is a stupid question…" began Ella.

"They're often the ones that get the best answers!" Elsie Knowle smiled. "Fire away!"

"Where is Kennaway Coopers. Is it in Ottery?"

"Have you found the Finnimore Industrial Estate near the old station?"

"We know where the old station is," replied Frank with a knowing look.

"Well, Kennaway Coopers is down there. They moved from their smaller old buildings about fifteen years ago. They're near the auction rooms."

"We've never come across the auction rooms or the industrial estate. I think we're due a walk around the town!"

※

That evening Frank and Ella did some research on walks around Ottery. The old Tourist Information website was gone but they did find a lot of information on one of Ottery's most famous sons– Samuel Taylor Coleridge.

"There are a couple of walks that take in various haunts of Coleridge when he was a boy," Frank observed as he checked out the pages of the Coleridge Memorial Trust website.

"I bet they don't go past the industrial estate!"

"No, he was about two centuries too early!"

"Well, I've found a town walk which combines Coleridge and the modern-day Ottery," said Ella.

"I'll print it out. What's the website address?"

Ella showed him the address from her iPad.

"Let's try it out tomorrow." Frank spent the rest of the evening reading up about Coleridge and Ottery St Mary so that he was ready to dispense various pearls of wisdom on the morrow!

❧

The morning dawned bright and cheerful. Another Devon cloudless sky. A good day for a good walk.

"We still haven't looked at the third clue," Ella recalled as they finished breakfast.

"Have you still got the piece of paper with it on?"

"Of course, I'm not throwing that away!"

"Well, write it down on another scrap of paper and we'll see if inspiration hits us as we walk."

Frank and Ella kitted themselves out for a gentle stroll around the town and then drove from Otterbury into Ottery St Mary. They parked in the Land of Canaan car park.

"Let's follow the walk from here. Where's your printout?"

Frank retrieved it from a jacket pocket, and they decided to follow the map in an anti-clockwise direction.

"We'll start by crossing the Coleridge bridge and then wander through the housing estate by the hospital."

They went back to the main road and then turned into the walkway down to the bridge. On their left was an empty children's playground. As Ella was looking across, she noticed the kerbstones on her left-hand side.

"What are these stones?"

"Where?"

"All along the path! It's a poem."

"Who do you think could have written the words?"

"That's pretty obvious–Coleridge. Samuel Taylor Coleridge. It's Kubla Khan."

"Here's the first verse." Frank read the famous opening words:

> *"In Xanadu did Kubla Khan*
> *A stately pleasure-dome decree:*
> *Where Alph, the sacred river, ran*
> *Through caverns measureless to man*
> *Down to a sunless sea."*

They followed the granite stones through its three verses as the path ran towards a bridge. They murmured the word to themselves until they reached the last lines of the final verse. Ella stopped and read them aloud:

> *"I would build that dome in air,*
> *That sunny dome! those caves of ice!*
> *And all who heard should see them there,*

And all should cry, Beware! Beware!
His flashing eyes, his floating hair!
Weave a circle round him thrice,
And close your eyes with holy dread
For he on honey–dew hath fed,
And drunk the milk of Paradise."

"But what does it mean? Is there a meaning to it?" Ella stood by the last stones and looked back along the path.

Frank gazed back as well. "It seems like a dream. He's obviously imagining a place called Xanudu."

"Is that Kubla Khan speaking in this last verse? I wonder if he's related to Genghis Khan? And those people, here at the end, appear to be scared of him. Perhaps they think he is a god or is invincible because he's drunk the milk of paradise?"

"You can see why so many people consider it a masterpiece," contemplated Frank.

"It's amazing to think it was written over two hundred years ago!"

"It would make a great science–fiction film," enthused Frank. "The CGI would really make it epic!"

"What's CGI?"

"Computer generated imagery. You know, an actor could be standing in a studio somewhere in London and the CGI could make it appear as if he is positioned in the middle of a lunar landscape."

"I'm happy to be just standing here with you. I don't need CGI for that!"

They stayed there for a silent moment before moving on, over a small bridge. They followed the path until they reached the footbridge over the River Otter. The path ran on to their right.

"Here's the industrial estate. Right in front of us." Ella exclaimed.

"Left, or right?" The tarmacked path seemed to lead to a housing estate.

"Left. I bet there's a path leading into the industrial estate.

It did.

"There's Kennaway Coopers."

The large sign rather gave the game away. Work appeared to be going on as usual.

"Do we go in and introduce ourselves?" Frank pondered.

"No. Let's wait until we're invited."

"Show a bit of respect?"

"Exactly."

They skirted the works and continued through the estate.

"Have you got the third clue with you?"

"Of course." Ella plucked it out of a pocket, turned it the correct way around and read: "*Go cross the bridge, I bid you well, To find a lot of mine won't sell.*"

Frank nodded. "The bridge could be the one we've just crossed, or it could be the road bridge. They both lead here."

Ella stopped and clapped her hands before pointing ahead. "Look! Auction Rooms. Ottery Auction Rooms! Bids.A lot of mine won't sell. We've solved our third clue."

"Let's hope it's the final clue."

Ella grabbed Frank's hand. "We need to ask what they do with the auction lots that don't sell."

"Don't the people who put them up for auction take them away again?"

"Perhaps. Maybe some don't get collected."

They went through the small door into the building.

They saw a stout, elderly man working in what they assumed to be the office.

"Excuse me," asked Ella, "is the auctioneer in the building?"

"No, she's out Axminster way." His accent was thick Devonian. "But I'm in charge. Arthur Sellars at yer service. 'Ow can I help 'ee?"

Frank clarified the reason for their presence in the building. "We've come to claim a beer barrel."

"You be wanting Kennaway Coopers for that. They be round the corner."

"No, it's a miniature beer barrel with some documents inside it," explained Frank.

Ella joined in. "It may have been left unsold from a recent auction."

"No beer barrels. But we did 'ave this envelope. Are you from Master Kennaway?"

"Well, yes."

"I need to see your letter. 'E said it would be green and scalloped!" Arthur held out his hand awaiting the letter.

"I left that at home. But the clue said: *Go cross the bridge, I bid you well, To find a lot of mine won't sell.*" Ella waved, in front of his face, the piece of paper with the clue on it.

"We crossed the footbridge and you accept bids. We need to find a lot that won't sell."

"Why won't 'ee sell?"

"Because you were told not to put it in the auction but to wait for it to be claimed."

"Exactly. Well done. 'Ere it be!"

Arthur turned around and fiddled with the mechanism to a small safe. Eventually, it opened, and he drew out another envelope.

"Another clue. Yippee!" muttered Frank with a look of disgust. "By the time we find the beer barrel, the documents will have crumbled away with age."

Arthur excitedly demanded: "Well, open it. Let us know what it says!"

Ella took out the green piece of scalloped paper and unfolded it. She read out the contents: "I planted this particular clue in the White's hydrangea's blue."

"Oh, that be eeezee!" cried Arthur.

"Oh, well what does it mean?"

"I'm not telling 'ee. Where would be the fun in that, m'dears."

Frank and Ella turned to each other with smiles of doleful resignation on both of their faces.

"Thank you very much for your help, Mr. Sellars."

"That's what neighbours be for, innit?"

"Neighbours?"

"I get this feeling in me bones that we'll soon be good neighbours."

෴

Frank and Ella made their way out of the industrial estate and across St Saviour's Bridge and along Mill Street back towards the town centre. Opposite the Methodist Church, Frank stopped and read the blue plaque on the wall of a square brick house.

"Raleigh House. It's said that Sir Walter Raleigh once lived on the site of this house. There was an earlier house, but it was burnt down in 1805. Edward Davy was born here in 1806. He invented a telegraph relay, a switch they later used in telephone exchanges."

Ella nodded but it was obvious her energy was flagging. "Before we go anywhere else, I need a cup of tea and a sit down," she groaned, "We seem to be going around in circles."

They soon found their favourite tea-shop. The husband and wife team who ran the place greeted them with a cheery smile. Frank and Ella were pleasantly surprised to find their favourite table was free. They sat down and breathed huge sighs.

"What did we miss by turning into Finnimore Estate?"

"Oh, just the hospital and a modern housing estate."

"No more doctors, please," shuddered Ella.

Frank ordered tea and cake.

"What's left on our town tour?"

Frank handed the map over to Ella.

"Market Square. The church. Jesu Street. And that's it."

"Yes, the rest of our walk is in Coleridge country."

"I think almost all of Ottery is Coleridge country!"

"Well, no. There was Raleigh and Edward Davy. Then there's the Tar Barrels and the Pixie Caves."

"True. It's not a one-horse town!"

They continued to enjoy the ambience of the tea shop–a pleasant murmur of chatter, the clink of cups and saucers, the occasional ringing of the old fashioned cash register and the regular tinkling of a bell as the shop door opened and closed. They were quietly talking about how it took them back to younger times when tea shops were a regular holiday haunt on seaside rainy days. Their children learned a lot of their social etiquette and their public table manners from such excursions.

Both Frank and Ella were jolted out of their reverie by the presence at their table of Kenneth Kennaway. He looked wary and a little frightened.

"Hello. Whatever is the matter?" Ella asked.

"May I talk to you?"

"Of course, grab a chair and sit down."

Kenneth took a spare chair from the adjoining table.

"Cup of tea? We can easily squeeze another out of this huge teapot."

"Yes, please. Milk and three sugars."

Ella went over to the counter to ask for an extra cup. She was back almost immediately.

"The sugar's there, by your elbow," motioned Frank.

Ella poured the tea and passed it across to Kenneth who picked the three largest lumps of sugar from the bowl and dropped them in.

Sugar was stirred and Kenneth still looked shaken.

"Have you been to see Kennaway Coopers yet?"

"No, we passed it by just now, but didn't think we should visit without an invitation."

"Oh, that's silly. You need to visit. I'll phone them and let them know you're going to visit."

"When?"

"Oh, just turn up. You'll want to see it on an ordinary working day, not a set-up performance!"

"Thanks, we'll do that."

"It's good to see some good coming out…. I mean, who would do such a…I'm sure they think…" Kenneth stuttered and stumbled over his words as he stared morosely into his cup of tea.

"There's something troubling you, isn't there?" said Frank in an obvious manner.

"No. Er-yes, it's that interview."

"At Kennaway Court?"

"Yes, I'm sure that those two police officers suspect me."

"To be fair, I think they suspect all of us," Frank responded gently.

"Not you. I don't know why you were there. But they've got it in for me. The trouble is, they may have a case."

"What do you mean?"

"Well, I may have pushed Dad through the bannisters… and down to his… death."

"What makes you say that?"

"I was totally out of it. I always drink too much when the pressure's on."

Ella felt sorry for the boy. She hoped her apprehension was not misplaced. "Do you remember anything?" she asked.

"No, that's the problem. I mean, Mum's a tough old cookie. She's as strong as anything but she wouldn't kill her own husband, would she?"

"Stranger things have happened," murmured Frank.

"And I saw both Carl and Fabian, Mr Cooper and Mr Fassbender, leave the premises. How could they have got back in without ringing the front door bell? I heard that lady sergeant say there was no sign of a break-in."

"So?"

"So, if they didn't do it, then I must have. I must have killed him. But I don't remember a thing."

"Have you a history of sleepwalking?" inquired Frank.

"Sleepwalking?"

"Yes, it's a common problem with stressed individuals."

"I don't… well, I'm told by Mum, and Dad, that I used to sleepwalk when I was a youngster. They told me they found me out of bed. Sleeping by the door. I even took my pillow with me."

"Interesting," mumbled Frank.

"Interesting? Are you mad?" Kenneth stared across the room.

"I've just realised. It could convict me!"

Kenneth spoke in short sentences scattered in between thoughtful silences.

"Oh no. This is dreadful. I've got to get away."

Neither Frank nor Ella said a word. They just listened.

"You haven't seen me. You don't want to see me. You mustn't get involved with a murderer."

He slurped the rest of his tea.

"What have I done?"

Kenneth staggered to his feet, knocking over his chair. He turned to go, bumped into the adjoining table and grabbing hold of the table cloth pulled it clean off the table. Cutlery, condiments and crockery went everywhere.

"Aargh. Now what? Sorry. Must be going. Oh, this mess, send the bill to…."

He stumbled through the tea shop, jerked open the door and shouted as he left: "Send it to Kennaway Court!"

"Excuse me, sir and madam." The female owner rushed up to Frank and Ella. "My husband and I couldn't help overhearing what young Mr Kennaway said. The whole shop heard it. We knew that Caleb Kennaway died, but we didn't know it was murder! We all heard that poor boy confess. You must call the police. You've just been taking tea with a murderer!"

Chapter Eight

Like one, that on a lonesome road
Doth walk in fear and dread,
And having once turned round walks on,
And turns no more his head;
Because he knows, a frightful fiend
Doth close behind him tread.

Frank and Ella knew they couldn't finish the town walk today so they paid the bill, thanked both of the cafe owners for their comments and assured them that they would phone Sergeant Knowle as soon as they reached home.

They kept to their word.

"Kenneth Kennaway made the same sort of comment at the end of his interview with me." Sergeant Knowle told them. "However, I want to wait until the DNA results come in to make sure."

"He's not a danger to anyone else, is he?" Frank asked.

"I don't think so. Were you in any way frightened or threatened by him?"

"No, not at all. I felt sorry for him," added Ella. They were using the speaker-phone so Frank and Ella could both hear what Elsie had to say.

"I'll badger someone for the results and then we'll take action. If they've found a ton of his DNA on Caleb's clothes, then I think Kenneth is our man. Until then, just lie low and go about your normal business."

"Yes, we've got another clue to solve."

"Not involving the Kennaway Court crime?"

"No, the Kennaway Coopers treasure hunt."

"Well, don't get the two mixed up."

※

With a cup of coffee, some hobnob biscuits and the sun shining onto Mutter's Moor they studied the latest clue.

"I planted this particular clue in the White's hydrangea's blue."

"Hydrangea is obvious. They're all over the place, though. Somewhere in Ottery has blue hydrangeas and the clue is planted in amongst them."

"Clue," groaned Frank. "Another clue. Not a miniature beer barrel or a casket that contains documents. No! Just another clue!"

"White's?"

"That can't be a colour or species of flower. Google White's of Ottery and see what comes up!"

"Gumtree. Amazon. White's Devon Directory of 1850."

Ella moved over to read: "Ottery Saint Mary is an ancient and irregularly built market town, of about 3500 inhabitants, picturesquely seated on the east side of the river 0tter, sheltered on the east and west by boldly swelling hills…"

"They've spelt Otter with a zero rather than an O! Typical." Frank was a stickler for good grammar, correct spelling and accurate labelling. It was, in fact, what started them off as amateur detectives in the first place.

"Two bedroom cottage for sale. Look at the next entry!" Ella exclaimed.

"Otter Garden Centres. Founded in Ottery St Mary when Malcolm and Marilyn White began growing vegetables and plants."

"Malcolm and Marilyn White. The White's of Ottery. And I bet they sell blue hydrangeas."

"They've got a cafe serving delicious home-made food."

"Guess where we're going for lunch."

⁓⁕⁓

Otter was the name of the garden centre. It was situated on the other side of Ottery St Mary between the town and the old A30 road. The sprawling garden centre spanned both sides of the road and was rather bigger than they expected. So was the cafe. However, the food was delicious and although the prices were a little more expensive than they were used to, they enjoyed their meal.

"I thought it was called Otter Nurseries," queried Frank.

"Yes, but all the branding just says Otter! They've lost the nurseries."

"I hope they haven't lost the blue hydrangeas."

Frank and Ella finished their food and sat there, engaged in one of Ella's favourite pastimes–people watching. There were groups of elderly citizens tottering from the self-service counter to their tables. They spied the occasional exhausted mum sipping some form of coloured water with their baby fast asleep in a pushchair or pram. "Luckily the little one's asleep. A precious few minutes of peace and quiet."

A couple of suited workers sat with smartphones in hand partaking in a midday meal away from the office. "Must be from Ottery," said Frank. "It's only a mile down the road."

"Look! Over there in the corner. Isn't that Kenneth Kennaway?"

"Not again!" muttered Frank.

"Yes, it's definitely him. He's trying not to see us."

"But we can see him. Elsie said we had to avoid contact with him until she's seen the DNA results."

They finished off their drinks.

"Let's go blue hydrangea hunting," Ella said with a twinkle in her eye.

They gathered their coats together, took their tray to the collection point. Ella couldn't resist another look across at Kenneth.

"He's gone. He's not there at his table."

"Good. It was probably just a strange coincidence."

They wandered out of the cafe and into the sunny outdoors. They made their way over to the plants and flowers section in search of the hydrangeas. There were not very many and, what there were, appeared to be pink or red. At the back of the section they saw a small wooden stake hammered into the ground. Attached to it was a picture of a blue hydrangea labelled *hydrangea cultivar*–Nikko Blue.

Ella looked all around her. "That's the only blue hydrangea I can see and it's not even real!"

"No, but there's a sticker attached to it. It's got the Kennaway Coopers logo."

Frank reached through the red hydrangeas and pulled the stake out of the earth. Ella took it from him. "The sticker says, '*The clue is in the office*'."

"Not another riddle?"

"No! I think we're meant to find the manager's office!"

Ella turned around to look for the office, but her eyes immediately tracked Kenneth Kennaway walking slowly down the roses section. He stopped every now and then to sniff the scents. Ella tapped Frank on the arm. "Don't look now, but Kenneth is in the vicinity. He's making it appear as if he's interested in the roses, but I'm convinced he's more interested in us."

Ella desperately resisted the temptation to walk over to him and ask "Can I help you?" Instead, she held on to Frank's hand and followed him towards the indoor section of the plant section where they had both seen the sign for customer services.

"Can we see the manager, please?" asked Frank.

"Oh, is there something wrong? Can I help?" The pleasant lady standing behind the blue veneered counter smiled.

"No, there's nothing wrong. We had a message to see the manager in their office." Ella smiled back.

"Hold on, I hope he isn't too busy."

He wasn't too busy. He soon appeared strolling behind the customer service lady.

"Good afternoon. My name's Harry Baker. I'm the manager. May I be of assistance?"

"Yes," said Frank. "We've come here to find a blue hydrangea. There's a clue in the office for us."

"That Caleb Kennaway and his sense of humour. He does like his jokes."

"Did like," retorted Ella.

"Yes, sorry, I forgot. Did like. It's such a pity he died. He was looking forward to retirement so much. He had great plans for that huge garden at Kennaway Court."

"Yes, it's a sad story," reflected Frank.

"Are you the treasure seekers?"

"I suppose we are," replied Ella.

"Follow me!"

He led them through the check-out counters and across the courtyard laden with stone statues and earthenware vases. They walked back towards the cafe. However, just before they got there, the manager turned sharply to his right, and led them up some stairs to his office.

"Have a seat. Sorry about the mess. My secretary's on holiday this week and I'm not too tidy when it comes to paperwork."

Harry Baker reached behind him and opened a small safe set into the wall beside a window that looked out over the courtyard towards the main entrance. He took out an envelope.

"Don't tell me," muttered Frank, "another clue?"

Ella laughed with a touch of desperation. "One of these days we'll run out of clues and actually find the treasure!!"

The manager handed over the envelope to Ella. "I remember you at Kennaway Court when you won the Ottery Lottery. Are you enjoying the treasure hunt?"

Ella smiled gratefully. "Well, we've not had time yet to enjoy it. It's been a hectic time. What with Caleb's death and…."

She stopped talking. Frank glanced sideways at her and noticed she was staring out of the window down into the courtyard.

"What's the problem, dear?" asked Frank.

"It's that boy again. Kenneth Kennaway. He's standing over there. On the far side of the courtyard by the stone bird tables."

"He's following us. I wonder if he's after the deeds?" Frank pondered aloud.

"Is he waiting for us to reach the end of the rainbow and then he'll claim the pot of gold for himself?" mused Ella, turning to her husband.

"Let's go and find out," decided Frank.

"Good idea!"

Frank turned to the office manager. "Thank you for your part in this treasure hunt. I'm sorry that we have to leave so quickly. Perhaps when Ella starts running the firm, we may be able to do some business?"

"I'd like that. I've always loved the style of those barrels. I could see us selling quite a few of them."

He showed them out, down the stairs and into the courtyard. Frank and Ella looked around but there was no sign of Kenneth Kennaway. Ella clutched hold of the envelope and they headed for their car parked in the main car park across the road.

☙❧

"Can we go for a little pootle to clear our heads." Ella appealed to her husband who nodded as he dropped into the driver's seat. They headed away from Otter on the winding Gosford Road, crossed under the new A30 bridge at Patteson's Cross and headed towards Feniton.

"I wonder who Patteson was?" contemplated Ella.

"That's strange," replied Frank. "I read about that only the other day. It seems that John Patteson was the son of Frances Coleridge and Sir John Patteson of Feniton Court. He became a missionary in the South Pacific and was killed by Solomon Islands natives who mistakenly thought his group were a raiding party looking for slaves. They put up this monument to him in 1873."

Ella was impressed.

Frank, however, was now watching his rear–view mirror. He began slowing down.

"What's the matter?" Ella asked.

"We're being followed."

"No need to ask who by."

"Exactly. Why would Kenneth want to follow us? Hold on!"

The car behind them pulled alongside. Frank swerved to the left to avoid a collision on the narrow road. The driver waved goodbye and then shot ahead at a speed totally unsuited for such a road.

"That was Kenneth Kennaway alright."

"Well, he's gone now."

Frank continued to meander through the village of Feniton with its influx of modern houses, over the level crossing by the station and then onwards to Colestocks. The road entering the village was bordered by a sturdy stone wall. They turned right by the whitewashed thatched house.

"Was that a Devon longhouse?" mused Frank as they left the village and headed up the narrow straight road towards the A373 Cullompton to Honiton road. Grass started to appear growing in the middle of the road and a deep ditch ran along the right-hand edge of the narrowing road. They drove down over a slight incline and curve and saw a car upturned in the ditch. The engine was smoking profusely. "Oh, my word," gasped Ella. "Stop! Stop! We must see if we can help."

Frank drove by and pulled to a halt about a hundred yards further down the road by a gateway of an isolated house. As he got out of the car, he heard a loud crack and then there was a horrific explosion as the car was engulfed in flames and thick black smoke.

"That was Kenneth's car, wasn't it?" shouted Ella.

"It looked like that. Call the police and the fire brigade. I'm going to see if…"

"No, Frank, no! Stay here. I'll phone but you stand still. Completely still"

Ella's tone of voice brought Frank to a complete halt. She meant business. He rarely heard her speak with such authority and passion. He just stood there knowing that there was nothing he could do to help whoever had been in the car. A second crack and explosion shook the ground and Frank staggered backwards and leant against the rear of his car. He could feel the heat of the fire from here. No-one could survive that.

Without taking in the actual content, Frank could hear Ella's words as she calmly spoke to whoever had answered her 999 call. Then she climbed out of the car and came to stand beside him. She put her arm around his waist and held him tightly.

"His poor mother," she whispered.

Chapter Nine

For not a hidden path, that to the shades
Of the beloved Parnassian forest leads,
Lurked undiscovered by him

The fire brigade arrived within ten minutes. "You were quick!"

"We had just finished up a fire at Payhembury. This is on our way home!"

The foam extinguishers soon put out the fire. The surrounding hedge and grass exposed the charred skeleton of the vehicle as it lay in ruins in the ditch.

Frank and Ella stood by their car and just watched the firemen in action. One of the fire officers approached them. "Good afternoon. I'm Fire Officer Whimple. I'm the leading officer."

Frank and Ella hardly responded. They continued staring at the burnt out vehicle.

"Are you OK? Which of you was in the car?"

Frank shook his head. "No. Neither of us. We came along and saw it in the ditch. Just as we were phoning 999 the thing exploded into flames."

Ella whispered, "We think we may know who was in the car."

"I think you'd better leave that to us," announced PC Hydon. Unnoticed by neither Frank nor Ella, the police had arrived in the hefty form of PC Hydon.

He led them away to his vehicle. They sat in the back seats and recounted to PC Hydon the events of the past few hours since they had arrived at Otter Nurseries.

"So 'ee think that Kenneth Kennaway may be the driver of that there car?"

"Yes, we're as certain as can be."

"Right, stay here for a few minutes whilst I be talking to these fire officers."

Earnest conversations took place between PC Hydon and Fire Officer Whimple, the man who had first spoken to them. PC Hydon took off his head–wear and scratched his head. They both walked around the car and then scrambled through the blackened hedge before searching around in the field. There were about thirty sheep in the field, but they had all moved to the farthest corner, well away from the gap in the hedge.

After ten minutes PC Hydon returned to the police vehicle and sat in the driver's seat.

"Well, I'll be Tom Pearced! This be a strange one."

"Is something wrong?"

"Well, yes. There be no driver. No body. No sign of anyone in or near the car."

"Could the explosion have completely disintegrated the body?" asked Frank.

"I asked that, and the answer is no. There's always some remains left behind. This time there's nothing."

"So, the driver, whoever he is, escaped before the car went up in flames?" questioned Ella.

"That, at the moment, is the probable explanation. Sometimes people get blown out of vehicles and are found nearby but we searched the field."

"What about the other side of the road?" asked Ella innocently.

PC Hydon opened the door and ran down the road, back towards the burnt-out car. He shouted at two firemen who crossed the road and clambered over a five-barred metal gate into another large field of grass. There were no sheep in the field. Frank and Ella got out of the police car to see what they might find. There was nobody in the field.

Frank looked around. A hedge dividing two fields ran at right angles to the road. It eventually led to an area of woodland about a quarter of a mile away. "What about the wood?" he shouted. PC Hydon and the two firemen moved as quickly as they could following the line of the hedge. Reaching the trees, they began searching methodically. They started at the nearest westerly edge and emerged a good fifteen minutes later at the far end. PC Hydon held something aloft and waved it towards Frank, Ella and the remaining firemen. Fire Officer Whimple gestured to two more of his colleagues and they started running towards the wood.

Another ten minutes passed before the group of five made their way back to the road. When they arrived, it was obvious to everyone that PC Hydon was carrying a rifle.

"Someone has been using this recently. We found it discarded in the middle of those trees."

Frank stepped forward. I thought I heard a crack before each of the explosions. It may well have been a rifle shot."

Ella asked: "Could anyone have set off an explosion by shooting at the car?"

One of the younger-looking firemen piped up, "It depends what they hit. If they were aiming for the petrol tank, then yes."

Another of the firemen added, "I saw what appeared to be the remains of a large petrol can scattered in the hedge."

"Go and collect any bits you can find," commanded Fire Officer Whimple.

"Did the driver set fire to his own car and then disappear into thin air?" wondered Ella.

"Or was someone waiting in the wood or better still behind that hedge…" began Frank.

"Deliberately waiting to kill the driver?"

"Well, I'll be clotted, that sounds like murder," said PC Hydon.

Fire Officer Whimple summed up their thoughts succinctly. "This incident has just become a whole lot more complicated."

❧

Frank and Ella followed PC Hydon back to Honiton and spent an hour in a musty room making a full statement about the accident. It was late afternoon before they had finished, signed their statements and were allowed home.

"Life is never dull in Devon." Frank and Ella were eating homemade shepherd's pie at their solid wooden table in the dining room.

"You know, so much happened this afternoon that we never even opened the envelope," exclaimed Ella.

"Where is it?"

"Still in my jacket pocket. I'll get it after we've eaten."

Twenty-five minutes later the washing up was completed and Frank and Ella sat down each with a cup of tea. Ella retrieved the envelope and extracted from it the folded green scalloped paper.

"Read out the next episode of the treasure seekers then," chuckled Frank.

"This is strange. I don't even know how to pronounce the first word. *Ptolemaic cosmology? Transept south is the place to be.*"

"Wait a minute. I'll Google it."

Frank quickly found a YouTube video on how to pronounce Ptolemy.

"Toll… Oh… Me…" said the gentleman at the YouTube channel PronunciationBook.

"A silent P."

"Wasn't Ptolemy some sort of Greek mathematician?"

"Yes, he lived in Egypt during the second Century. According to the Encyclopaedia Britannica he modelled the Ptolemaic system where Earth is the centre of the universe. Our planet was thought to be stationary with everything else in the universe revolving around us. It says that Ptolemy was responsible for this geocentric cosmology being followed in the Islamic world and in medieval Europe."

"Ptolemaic cosmology? Everything revolves around the earth. Now the Science Museum in London would have something about this surely?"

"Just looking it up as you speak."

"Hurry up!"

Frank grimaced. "Yes, your highness!"

"Hey, if we solve this clue, you may have to call me boss!"

"So, what's changed!"

"Cheek!"

"Here we go. In the Science Museum blog, it says Claudius Ptolemy was a Roman citizen who wrote in Greek and lived in Alexandria. His theory was the accepted model for over 1400 years."

Frank went quiet as he began typing away into Google again.

"Cracked it!"

"How?"

"I typed Ottery St Mary Ptolemaic cosmology and guess what's top of the rankings?"

"Not a clue!"

"The south transept houses the Ottery St Mary Astronomical Clock, one of the oldest surviving mechanical clocks in the country."

"Brilliant. That's the clue. But where is this clock?"

"In the church. In the south transept. The transept runs at right angles to the nave in any church. If the church were shaped like a letter t then the transept is the short line crossing the main stem."

"It's so obvious once you think about it. Another trip into Ottery tomorrow. This time to church. Will the church be open? It's not Sunday."

"I'm sure it will be. If not, someone will know who the churchwardens are."

"So, there'll be another clue somewhere around this clock?"

"I don't think the church would have given Caleb permission to dig a hole in the transept and bury his barrel in it!"

"Don't tell me anything else about the church or the clock or the transept. My brain's on overload after all the events of today. Let's switch on the TV and watch Death in Paradise, one of the older episodes. I hope you haven't deleted any of them off the HD box."

"Wouldn't dare!"

༺༻

The next day they ambled into Ottery, parked in their usual space in their usual car park and wandered up to the church. As they walked up Gold Street, a large car drew up alongside them. "Mr and Mrs Raleigh, I presume."

Both Frank and Ella turned towards the open window of the four-wheel drive.

"The Zummerset Zyder Mafia!"

"At your service," squeaked a voice from the back seats of the car which Ella immediately recognised as Delbert Fitzpaine.

"Be quiet in the back," commanded Albert Fitzhead. "We've been attempting to meet up with Christine and Kenneth Kennaway to conduct some business but they're not at home to visitors."

"How can we help?"

"Well, if you're conducting your usual enquiries then perhaps there's some information that we'd like to share with you."

Frank nodded. "Why not park this monstrosity and meet us at the Kings Inn." He pointed to the pub further along Gold Street.

"Will do," agreed Norbert Fitzwarren, the driver.

Frank and Ella walked across to the Kings Inn, found a quiet table and ordered a pot of coffee and a pot of tea.

"Shouldn't take too long and then we'll go and see that clock."

A couple of minutes later, as the tea and coffee were being placed on their table, in walked the three gentlemen. As usual, they were dressed in similar dark suits and yet again, they reminded both Frank and Ella of the sketch in the Frost Report with John Cleese, Ronnie Barker and Ronnie Corbett.

They all sat down.

"Thank you for the refreshments," said Albert.

"I'll pay for them when we leave," volunteered Norbert.

Delbert poured teas and coffees and passed them around to each person. The quintet supped in silence.

"How can we help you?" began Ella.

"Well, we have a confession to make."

"As long as it doesn't involve cider consumption," recalled Frank.

"Sorry about that. We didn't totally trust you at the time. Now we do," replied Albert.

"Tell us about your confession," asked Ella.

"It's about the evening that Caleb Kennaway died," commenced Albert.

"We were there!" interrupted Delbert.

"In the house?"

"No, not quite. We have an ongoing business discussion with the family, and we had spent the day in the area up at Sowden Valley Farm. We thought we'd call in and see how things were going."

"We arrived outside the house and stood at the front door preparing to knock." Albert paused for effect.

"When we heard an almighty row going on in the hallway," interrupted Delbert.

"They was going hammer and tongs. We could hear every word," expressed Norbert.

"We didn't want to jump into the middle of a heated discussion. Business dealings should be conducted in a formal genteel atmosphere."

"So, we scarpered!" shouted Delbert.

The other customers in the Kings Inn all turned towards them.

Delbert stood up and faced them. "Sorry," he grinned, bowed to the other customers and then resumed his seat.

"Have you told the police this information?"

"No, we thought discretion might be the better part of valour."

"And anyway," added Norbert, "nobody knew we were there until we realised, we might have a problem."

"What was that?" asked Frank.

"It seems that Norbert may have driven rather too fast through a speed trap. It was set up just outside Ottery St Mary."

"We received the speeding ticket this morning in the post!" Norbert glumly communicated.

"So, putting two and two together, we thought that that lady police sergeant might wonder why we were in Ottery on the evening of Caleb's death."

"Caleb's murder, we think," added Frank.

"Oh, my word," gasped Albert, "That makes it even worse. I'm sure she is out to get us. We had so much trouble in Sidmouth last time. She's bound to remember all that fuss."

"Did you kill Caleb?" asked Ella.

"No, of course not. We wanted him alive. We wanted all the family alive. We had a very advantageous business deal coming our way. Why would we jeopardise that?"

"Can I ask what this deal was?"

"Yes, I suppose so. Christine Kennaway was negotiating with us to buy Taunton Norton Cider."

"What?"

"Yes, we're selling the business. We're going to retire."

Chapter Ten

*Water, water, everywhere,
And all the boards did shrink;
Water, water, everywhere,
Nor any drop to drink.*

"Selling. Retire? But why?" Frank and Ella were shocked.

"Well, Christine saw how well we were doing. And we've achieved so much in the past two years that it's time to sit back and decide what else we want to do with our lives."

Delbert leaned forward. "Also, Albert's getting married!"

Albert shushed Delbert and his face blushed a deep red.

"Congratulations," cried Ella.

"And before you make another comment, I'm not too old to get spliced."

"The thought hadn't crossed my mind," responded Ella, "everyone deserves a little happiness at whatever age Delbert thinks you are."

Norbert chortled. "You haven't met his intended! A little happiness, that's a good one."

Albert turned his head slowly towards Norbert who suddenly became very interested in the bottom of his coffee cup.

Ella and Frank quite enjoyed the repartee of the Taunton Norton trio, who continued to regale them with a wealth of stories stretching back decades illustrating the weird and wonderful aspects of the cider industry.

"Whatever happened to that farm out at Sowton?" asked Frank, knowing the answer but intrigued to find out a little background information.

"We bought it," said Delbert.

"I'd heard that," added Ella. "Was it a good buy?"

"It's been the best!" replied Norbert.

"What Norbert means is that it's enabled us to move on to the next stage of our lives–our retirement. It won't do any harm to let you know, but we completed a deal with a couple of supermarket chains to supply them with the cider."

"All over the UK!" chimed in Delbert.

"The most interesting thing is that we've supplied each of them with the same cider. They're promoting it with a different brand name, and each is advertising it as a rival commodity to the other. People will compare each of the brands, buy one of them and probably think their choice is better than the other brand. But we know, they're really just drinking the same cider–our cider!"

"And we've made a fortune out of it!" crowed Delbert.

Frank and Ella both chuckled. "I wonder how many other rival brands are exactly the same product?"

"Perhaps the basic baked beans and the high priced luxury baked beans are really one and the same!" Ella mused. "Sometimes too much choice is not good for us!"

"Do you know the difference between cider and scrumpy?" asked Delbert.

"Aren't they both just cider?" pondered Frank.

"Yes and no. Cider is filtered to a clear liquid and then loses some of its potency," replied Norbert.

"But, scrumpy is made with the apples that ain't good enough for cider," continued Delbert.

"A bit like the basic baked beans?" asked Ella.

"No, scrumpy is rough stuff, all cloudy with apple bits in it."

"And it'll give a guaranteed hangover if you drinks more than a little!" concluded Delbert.

"Is that what you gave me?" asked Frank remembering his pub crawl with the Zyder boys in Sidmouth.

"No, you just couldn't take your drink!" countered Albert.

All three laughed and smiled knowingly at Ella.

Morning coffee turned into an excellent ploughman's lunch, followed by clotted cream and fruit. By mid-afternoon Frank and Ella had completely forgotten why they had come to Ottery in the first place.

"We must be going," said Frank.

"So, must we," said Albert.

"I'll get the bill," added Norbert.

"Make sure you don't just get the bill but that you pay it as well!" cried Delbert.

Frank had deliberately drunk nothing more potent than orange juice this time. Ella had made a mild cider last most of the session, so they were able to regain their car and drive back to Otterbury in a sober but restful state of mind.

It was only as they sat down in the front room armchairs that Frank remembered: "We never got anywhere near the Astronomical Clock in the church."

"That will have to wait till another day. I'm not going back to Ottery again today. I'm stuffed and I refuse to budge one more inch."

They spent the rest of the day in Couch Potato Land bingeing on old episodes of Downton Abbey and The Crown.

❦

The following morning, before they were able to leave the house for Ottery, they received a visit from Sergeant Knowle.

"Come in. Is it Elsie or Sergeant Knowle?"

"It'll be Elsie, as soon as I'm inside admiring your view of Mutter's Moor and sitting with a cup of tea in my hand."

Frank went off to the kitchen to make tea.

"Make yourself comfortable. What brings you to our humble abode?"

"I've got some information that may make you feel better about the other day."

"You mean that horrible accident?"

"Yes, I'll just wait for Frank to come back in to save me repeating myself too much!"

Elsie sat there staring out of the window and letting the cares of the day disappear for a little while.

Frank brought in mugs of tea and a plate of biscuits.

"Right, Elsie, fire away," he said.

"A rather unfortunate turn of phrase," smiled Elsie.

"Sorry!"

"Kenneth Kennaway as far as we can ascertain is not dead."

Frank nodded. "Good. I hoped not."

"You mean?"

"I mean that I think he set fire to the car to make us think he was dead. To give him time to escape and maybe even leave the country."

"Why do you say that?" asked Elsie.

"He was a very scared man." Continued Frank, "I think he convinced himself that he killed his father. He may have done. Regardless of that, he cracked under the strain."

"Let me stop your thoughts right there for a minute. I think you may be right about the car. However, we've received the DNA reports back from our labs. We took samples from each of the four people there that night. And there's very little DNA from Kenneth on Caleb's clothes. The other three have DNA traces galore but not Kenneth. A good lawyer would get him off a murder charge with ease. The CPS wouldn't want to proceed with a case like that."

"So, is he innocent of the murder of Caleb?" asked Ella.

"In all probability, yes! However, we also found Mrs Kennaway's evening gloves in the compost bin around the back of the kitchen garden. Both Caleb's and her DNA were all over them. To add to that, fibres from Caleb's dressing gown were found on the gloves as well."

"That's interesting. But is that conclusive evidence?"

"Not yet, no. Now back to your guesswork, sorry, your deductions," smiled Elsie.

"I think Kenneth fired the shots that caused the car to explode. He fired from behind the hedge and escaped along the hedge and through the woods. By the time we searched the woods, he was long gone."

"I think you may be right. We've done a few background checks on the rifle. It belongs to the Kennaway family. Caleb held the licence. It was securely locked away in an inside room within Kennaway Court. It's not there now. "

"Well, it's good to hear he's still alive," stated a delighted Ella. "Does his mother know?"

"Not yet. When I called to check on the rifle she wasn't there. I'd like to see her reactions to the recent events."

"That's a bit cruel," said Ella.

"No, not if she's the murderer! But there's more."

"Don't tell me, you've caught Kenneth boarding a ferry at Plymouth?"

"No, unfortunately not. After the DNA results came in, I did some digging around. I contacted the local airports. No luck at Exeter, Bristol or even Newquay. So, I tried further afield."

"And he boarded a flight from Heathrow to Albania," cried Ella.

"How did you know?"

"His mother's charity was in Albania, wasn't it? He's gone into hiding in an area of the world where it would be quite difficult to trace him. Yes?"

"Spot on. He caught the last flight yesterday from Heathrow to Tirana in Albania. He used his real name and his own passport."

"Money?"

"I checked his bank accounts. He made a rather substantial withdrawal from one of them during yesterday."

"What do we do now?"

"Nothing much. We'll try to track him down. But he hasn't really committed an offence. I suppose setting your own car on fire is stupid and dangerous, but I don't think it would count as a crime."

"And then there were three," mused Frank.

"Maybe not," interrupted Ella. "We met three gentlemen yesterday in Ottery St Mary who wined and dined us and made great efforts to get us to look upon their plight with sympathy."

Ella explained about their meeting with Albert, Norbert and Delbert.

"The Zummerset Zyder Mafia are back in town," chuckled Elsie.

"And although it seems highly improbable that they would murder Caleb, we can't discount it."

"True. There was unidentified DNA on his clothes."

The conversation turned to more inconsequential matters until Elsie finished her tea and biscuits and bid them farewell. "I'll let you know when there's any further developments."

"Thank you. Now we've got a treasure hunt to complete!"

୨ৎ

When Sergeant Knowle had gone on her way, Ella suggested to Frank an agenda for the day. A trip to Ottery and a surprise visit to Kennaway Coopers followed by a look at the church clock. Both Frank and Ella had completed some background research on the church.

"I found out that the town's name, Oteri Sancte Marie, was first recorded in 1242 taking its name from the River Otter and its connection with Rouen Cathedral in France," said Ella.

"Good start. But did you know that work on the church began in 1342. Its design was deliberately made to look like Exeter Cathedral."

"Yes, and the north aisle was added in 1520."

"And that was the last addition," concluded Frank. "Oteri Sancte Marie. That sounds Latin but the manor lands round about here belonged to Rouen."

"Yes, I suppose that Latin was used because Rouen Cathedral is a Roman Catholic cathedral?"

"What about the clock?" Frank asked.

"No-one knows exactly how old it is but it is similar to a clock in Exeter Cathedral and that one dates from the 1400s."

"It must be old because it shows the medieval view of the universe where the sun rotates around the earth."

"And, I was reading, probably on the same website, that it was in 1543 that Copernicus stated that he thought that the model was the wrong way around and that the earth actually revolved around the sun." Frank stated knowledgeably.

"I know the clock is in the South transept."

"Below the bell tower!"

"We're so clever and well-read!"

"Amazing what the internet can teach you these days! If we were in a novel, they'd call that an information dump. It's meant to be bad but how can any sharing of such wonderful knowledge be bad?"

"I think," concluded Ella, with a huge smile upon her face, "it's time we went into Ottery. A visit to the company and then an actual look at that clock!"

❧❧

Frank and Ella turned up at Kennaway Coopers in an enthusiastic and amenable mood. They were determined to learn as much as they could about the art of cooperage.

They met up with the foreman, George Snook, who showed them quickly where the basic amenities were, before handing them over to two burly gentlemen

"These two will answer any of your questions," said George. "Ask them whatever you like! I'll be in the office when you're finished."

With that, the foreman swivelled on his heels and returned to the main office.

"I think we've met before," said Ella.

"Yes, you sold us the tickets that started the process that has brought us here this morning!" added Frank.

"Where are your baseball caps?"

"Ah, can't wear that those here! Anyway, welcome to Kennaway Coopers. I'm Josiah Cobden."

"And I be Terence Talaton. Terence, not Terry! We're the senior employees here at Kennaway Coopers."

"Yes, I remember. You both left school and have worked here ever since," recalled Frank.

"Can I just say, before we go any further, that if I'm to take on this place in the future, then I shall need some experienced support. I do not intend to sack any person in this place. I want to preserve and progress, not search and destroy!"

"We're right glad to hear that, ma'am!"

"We're very happy to support any person, whoever they may be," said Josiah, "who's willing to continue to build on our proven foundations! We have a tradition here that we're mighty proud of. We don't want to see it go to waste."

"My word," said Terence, "that's the most eloquent I've heard 'ee speak in nigh on twenty years."

"Yes, I knew our two visitors would come and see us sometime soon as I spent two hours last week working out what to say. I wrote it down on this piece of paper and memorised it!"

Josiah waved a scrap of paper around before screwing it up and stuffing it in his pocket.

"Bravo is what I say," cried Ella. "You've given me a reason to keep going." She beamed at both Josiah and Terence. "I think we're going to get along just fine!"

"Then we'd better show you around."

"The art of barrel making, or cooperage, as it should be known, started over 2000 years ago. There's evidence that the Romans used barrels in the third century."

Terence chipped in. "It's called cooperage after the Latin and German words for barrel–kupe or cupa."

"My word, you sound just like my husband!"

They had made their way into a large shed-like room with a fire in a small brazier in the middle. "Does it get cold in here," asked Frank.

"No, that's for the toasting," said Terence.

In front of them was one of the workmen. He was just beginning to assemble a new barrel.

Josiah continued. "As you can see here, barrels are made with staves and hoops. The staves are made of knotless oak that's been aged for about two or three years. They're cut to a uniform length, but they can be of varying widths."

"The hoops are made of metal and are used to hold the staves together," added Terence.

Josiah nodded. "The cooper inserts the staves inside the top hoop called the chime hoop. Most coopers use a pattern of narrow, medium and wide staves around the barrel to dissipate the forces. There can be as many as thirty staves used in a barrel."

Josiah appeared to be the main guide with extra snippets being provided by Terence. "We carve a little notch near the top and bottom of each stave called the croze groove. You'll see why later. Once all the staves are in place then another hoop called the quarter hoop is placed just below the chime hoop to hold the staves more securely."

"At this point, it looks like the petals of a flower. In fact, they call this part of the process *mise en rose* or setting the rose."

"The staves look like they're blooming out from the chime hoop," added Frank.

"When that's done the cooper will steam the wood to soften it and then use one of our cables to draw the wood into the proper shape at the foot of the barrel. When the cable is tightened and the staves are in place, we bind them with more hoops. The middle hoop where the barrel is at its widest diameter is called the bilge hoop. You'll notice the complete absence of glue or nails or screws."

"Now the whole thing looks like a barrel. But it's not finished yet."

"That's where the fire comes in. Each barrel is toasted over an open flame."

"Why?" asked Ella.

"Well, that's a good question. Some people swear that the wine or beer tastes better from a toasted barrel. The toasting releases the flavour. Others say it stops the woods from absorbing too much of the liquid. If too much air is left in a barrel, then the wine in the barrel used to turn to vinegar. In the early years of barrel-making the coopers toasted the wood to make the staves more pliable."

"Whatever the reason, we always toast each barrel. We use these small braziers and the skill is knowing when the wood is ready. Too much flame and the wood will burn. Not enough and the toasting is a waste of time."

"You two certainly know your trade," said Frank.

"Experience," replied Josiah.

"Is that the end of the process?" asked Ella.

"Oh no, Terence is the master of the next stage."

"My job," continued Terence, "is to make the head. There are two heads, one each at the top and bottom of the barrel. Each barrel is a unique shape, so each head has to be correctly measured and individually made. I shape the staves by an age-old process. It was passed down to me when I was a youngster by the senior header. I pass it on to the headers I train. When the head is ready, I sit them on the croze groove. And then my job is almost complete."

"Don't forget the bung-hole."

"Just coming to that, Josiah. I mill a bung-hole in the lower half of the barrel so we can get the wine or beer in or out of the barrel. We used to leave the bung-hole to the breweries to mill but it's easier to do it ourselves."

"What do you mean by mill?" asked Ella.

"That's the process of drilling or boring a hole. When everything's finished, we hammer in an oak bung."

"There's an awful lot of skill involved in making a barrel. Is that all?"

"No. Quality control is next. Come over here."

Josiah led them to the far side of the huge workroom. A large metal tank stood against the wall.

"Is there beer inside that tank?"

"No, it's good old fashioned water. We use a pipe to fill each barrel through the bung-hole. If it leaks, then it's a wasted barrel. I know, what you're gonna ask! We don't throw them away. We get out the fire again and heat the wood to fuse it. A well-made barrel will rarely need much work to make it waterproof."

"And we produce well-made, high-quality barrels! Look how dry the floor is!"

Josiah and Terence took them back to the workroom entrance.

Ella turned around to the other workmen in the workroom. "Thank you for putting up with our interruptions. What you're doing is an amazing skill–we have no intentions of stopping you working any further."

She turned to Josiah and Terence. "We can't thank you enough for your kindness. You explained everything so well. I really think I understand why this company needs to continue to use such skilled local workers. If I have any say in the matter, Kennaway Coopers has got a long and successful future stretching in front of it."

"I'm glad to hear that, ma'am," replied Josiah.

"You're both welcome to have a look around any time you like," added Terence.

"We'll take you back to George Snook in the office. You take good care of yourselves."

Josiah and Terence delivered them to the foreman in the main office. They spent the next few hours being shown order books, accounts, profit and loss spreadsheets. It was all very positive but both Frank and Ella found themselves becoming bamboozled and bombarded by information. Frank eventually called a halt.

"Thank you for your time. We've got a lot to think about. If things go according to plan, then we may see you again in the near future."

Ella again wanted to reassure the staff of Kennaway Coopers. "We have no intention of upsetting the apple cart. We want this company to continue serving the local community. But right now, we have an appointment with a clock."

Chapter Eleven

Dear native brook! wild streamlet of the West!
How many various-fated years have passed,
What happy and what mournful hours, since last
I skimmed the smooth thin stone along thy breast,
Numbering its light leaps!

The Astronomical Clock did not disappoint. Its blue face, with its two circular dials, had a golden ball representing the moving sun to show the time and a half black, half white ball to show the moon and its age and phases. A black sphere at the centre of the clock represents the earth.

"Absolutely incredible that a clock like that should be here." An elderly man stood beside them looking up at the clock. "It was a marvel of medieval mechanical craftsmanship!"

Ella agreed. "Yes, it must have made the town so proud to have something like that here in this church?"

"There's only one problem," said Frank.

"I know what you're going to say," said the gentleman. "Let me introduce myself. I'm Geoff Whittaker, one of the Church Wardens. What's the problem?"

"An envelope."

"Yes, somehow I knew it was you. I've been waiting for someone to ask me about it. Are you connected with poor Caleb?"

"Sort of," began Ella.

"Because I recognised you from the Lottery gathering in Kennaway Court. You won the Lottery, didn't you?"

"Yes."

"And Caleb asked us to stick that envelope up there until someone came along to ask for it."

"I hope it hasn't damaged the clock's casing?"

"No, the wonder of blutak!"

"Well, we'd like to have the envelope, please?"

"Caleb told me to ask you this question."

"Go on?"

"Where did you find the hydrangea and what colour was it?"

"Oh, that's easy. In Otters and it was blue–except they only had a picture of the blue ones. The real ones were either red or pink."

"That's the soil for you."

"Can we have the envelope?"

"Certainly. Let me find our ladder."

Within a few minutes, Ella had the envelope in her hand.

"Well, open it," said Geoff Whittaker.

Ella smiled and did so.

"Another clue. Is there an end in sight?"

"That makes six by my reckoning," agreed Frank.

"Aren't you going to read it?" urged the expectant churchwarden.

Ella read out aloud the next clue: "*A circle midst a miller's stream will house a box inside a screen.*"

"Tumbling Weir," said Geoff immediately.

"Tumbling Weir? I've heard of that. Isn't it somewhere here in Ottery?" Ella asked.

"Indeed!"

"But what is it?"

"It's a rare thing. A circular weir in a small mill pond that allows water to get back to the River Otter."

"How?" Ella was becoming interested.

"The water falls into a tunnel through a series of rings."

"But why didn't they just cut a channel back to the river?"

"The water in the millpond drove a water wheel and corn mill from the late 1700s. There wasn't enough water power from the leat so they raised the level of water in the millpond by about 8 feet to get the wheel turning."

"So?"

"If they just let the water go back to the river it would drain the leat and the pond. So that's why the weir is really an overflow. You need to go and see it. Then it'll be as clear as mud!"

Ella wasn't sure she understood the mechanics of it all. She turned to Frank. "Did you understand all that?"

Frank nodded solemnly. His hands were in his pockets with fingers crossed. He looked at Geoff Whittaker with a faint smile on his face. "How do you know so much about the Tumbling Weir?"

"I'm not only Church Warden but I'm a part-time guide when they do the guided tours of the town."

"Perhaps you should have won the Ottery Lottery!"

"No way, I'm too old to run a business. That's a young man's game."

"Hmmph!" grunted Ella.

"Pardon me, madame, a young person's game."

"I think that's a compliment." Ella's expression changed from a frown into a smile.

"You're as young as you feel. There's plenty more years in you before you claim your bus pass."

Ella beamed.

Frank interrupted, "How do we get to this Tumbling Weir?"

"Down Mill Street and through the new houses. Or you can go in Land of Canaan past the Coleridge Stones, cross the small bridge turn sharp left and follow the footpath."

"We know where the Stones are so we'll follow the footpath," said Frank. "Thanks for your help."

Ella chipped in: "Thank you for the information. You probably saved us a lot of time by solving this clue. Let's hope we're near the end of them all."

Frank and Ella turned to go.

"Good luck!" Geoff bade them farewell.

They wandered out from the church, back down the Silver Street hill, past the supermarket and into Land of Canaan.

"It seems a while since we stopped and read these stones." Ella stepped smartly past the granite poem.

"That must have been 3 clues ago!"

"How many clues have we solved so far?"

"Well, I think this one is the sixth."

"There can't be that many left."

"Well, at least the clues are proving our determination to run Kennaway Coopers."

Ella stopped and faced Frank. She reached out and held one of his hands. "Frank, I'm not sure I want to run this company."

"OK…."

"I mean I like the idea of keeping it going for the locals, but have I got the time and the energy?"

"I think that's for you to decide."

"Yes," said Ella thoughtfully.

"Well, in that case, do you want to go and see Christine and the other directors and let them know about this?"

Ella stood there cogitating. Thirty seconds went by in silence.

"No. Let's solve this clue. If it's the last one, then I'm the new owner. If it's not, well… either way we need to go and talk to Christine Kennaway and the others. Find out what they might want to do with the company now that Caleb's dead."

"You do realise we'll be negotiating with a murderer."

"You mean you don't think Kenneth is our man?"

"I have an open mind on the matter but no, I think he's a very scared young man. He's scared because he thinks he may have done it. I'm not so sure he did."

"I agree with you. I had a feeling he's just a youngster who needs to grow up. Perhaps escaping from here may be the making of him."

"On to the Weir?"

"Certainly. Let's go tumbling."

They found Tumbling Weir and faced a problem.

"*A circle midst a miller's stream then seek a box inside a screen.*" Ella read out the clue on the green scalloped paper.

"The circle in the middle of the mill stream's easy to locate. There it is. But a box?"

"We need help."

A shadow of a man crossed the path beside them.

Frank turned towards the newcomer. "Geoff Whittaker, how did you know…?"

"Are you some sort of guardian angel from the church?"

"Are you following us?"

"No, I live along here in one of the new houses. I'm just going home for my lunch."

"Well, perhaps you can help. Now we're here the second part of a clue is baffling us. It says…"

"*The box inside a screen*. That's easy. Last year, some people from the university placed a screen container here to measure the flow of the water. They put it on the first ledge. It's got a few devices attached to it and a lid for easy access."

"I bet there's a miniature beer barrel inside the screen container!" shouted Ella. "This is it!"

"How do we get across to the weir? Is it deep?"

"No, not really. But there's tangled weeds and stuff," cautioned Geoff.

"Couldn't I just put my wellington boots on and wade to the weir?"

"Do we need a boat?" said Ella.

"Well, there is one up by the leat." Replied Geoff. "They use it to unclog the weir when they do their maintenance. But no, I would think a pair of waders would do the trick."

"Where would I get waders?" queried Frank.

"Well…"

Ella smiled. "You've got some, haven't you, Mr Whittaker?"

Yes, I use them when I go fishing down on the River Dart."

"Can we borrow them, Mr Whittaker, please?" begged Ella.

~~

They all went along to Geoff's house and soon Frank was kitted out in a pair of musty green waders.

"Aren't you joining Frank, Mr Whittaker?" asked Ella.

"No, I've only got the one pair. You and I can stay on the bank just in case something goes wrong."

"Now, let me get this straight," said Frank. "All I have to do is wade across to the tumbling weir and check the screen to see what's inside?"

"That's right," replied Geoff. "You'll have to climb over the fence first of all. I'll bring you a small two-step ladder. Oh, and a long pole. I'll use the washing line pole. That should be ok."

Back at the Tumbling Weir, Frank climbed over the metal fence and gingerly stepped into the leat. He didn't sink in too far before he located the firm base. He made his way step by hesitant step towards the weir. Mr Whittaker held out the pole towards Frank.

"Just grab if you feel you're overbalancing!"

The leat water was imperceptibly moving towards the weir. There was hardly any overflow with little water tumbling over the edge. Frank looked over the side and could see the screen and its box within easy reach. Attached to the box was a plastic water bottle.

"Be careful," called Ella. "I don't want to lose you down the weir," she said.

"There's something here. On top of the box. It's a plastic bottle. Inside it is what looks like one of those envelopes. It's all wrapped up in plastic."

"I know," shouted Geoff Whittaker, "Caleb asked me to put it there a few weeks ago!"

"Why didn't you say?"

"Didn't want to spoil the fun!"

Frank carefully picked it up and turned around to make his way back towards the leat bank. As he did so, the increasing roar of a nearby plane caused all three to look around to see where the sound was coming from.

"That's low," shouted Geoff.

From over the roof of the houses a propeller-driven aircraft appeared. Only one of its two engines were working. The four propeller blades on the dead engine were clearly visible. The plane was flying so low that Ella could see the name Flybe on its fuselage. As it flew over, all three of them ducked as if it might hit them. In an instant, Ella's eyes took in the detailed picture. The plane was long and narrow with an engine below each wing. The wings were joined to the top of the fuselage giving it the appearance of an old bi-plane. She was sure she could see people looking out of the plane's windows.

Suddenly the roar ceased. Ella could see the other propeller slowing to a halt.

"It's going to crash, Frank!" she shouted.

"Frank?" Ella twisted around to talk to Frank, but he wasn't where she had last seen him. He had fallen over when he ducked and was floundering in the shallow leat, splashing around and desperately trying to hold the plastic bottle above the water.

"What are you doing?"

Geoff didn't know whether to continue watching the plane or run for help. Ella, with a presence of mind that later surprised her, caught hold of the washing line pole. She pointed it towards Frank who was still splashing around in the water.

"I've got my hand entangled in these weeds!"

Frank tugged and quickly untangled his hand from the weeds and grabbed the other end of the pole.

"Don't pull on the pole," cried Geoff, "you'll have her in there as well."

Chapter Twelve

Whom the untaught Shepherds call
Pixies in their madrigal,
Fancy's children, here we dwell:
Welcome, Ladies! to our cell.

Too late. Ella joined Frank in the water. She was soon standing in two foot of water whilst still holding onto the washing line pole.

Geoff stood by the millpond failing in his attempt to curtail his laughter.

Together they waded through the muddied waters of the leat towards the bank. Reaching it, they clambered out.

"So that's why they call it the Tumbling Weir!" she spluttered.

Frank and Geoff joined together in uncontrolled laughter. Ella soon succumbed.

"Come along! Quickly! Let's get you to my house and we'll soon have you warm and dry!"

"What happened to the plane?"

"I don't know. There are no plumes of smoke in the sky. Perhaps they restarted the engines?"

They arrived back at the Whittaker residence to be met at the front door by Mrs Whittaker. "Oh, Geoff, I've just seen the most extraordinary thing."

"Hold on, love. Tell us all about it after we get these two treasure hunters warm and dry."

❦

In no time at all, they were sat in the cosy front room of the Whittaker house drinking hot tea and listening to the sound of sirens rushing through Ottery.

"They're going to the aeroplane," announced Mrs Whittaker.

"Tell us all about it, love," asked Mr Whittaker.

"Well, I was upstairs doing some dusting in the back bedroom when I saw this plane flying over the house. It was so low, I felt I could reach out and touch it. I'm surprised it didn't knock our chimney off."

"We saw it too," added Ella.

"That's partly how these two ended up so cold and wet! Carry on."

"The plane glided around in a tight circle. It seemed as if the pilot was looking for a place to land. He seemed to pick a spot and lined the aeroplane up and descended towards one of the fields beside the river. It was so smooth and graceful. He didn't seem to lower the wheels. He just did a gentle belly flop. It slid over the field. I could see it all from the window."

"The plane didn't explode or anything?"

"No. When it stopped, I saw two doors open in the fuselage and passengers leaping down on what looked like a cross between a slide and a bouncy castle."

"Everyone got out alright?"

"Yes, everyone. When the passengers reached the ground, one of the stewards was gesturing at them to get up and run towards the path by the river. There was a herd in cows in the field. I've never seen cows run so fast in all my days!"

"What a miraculous escape for both man and beast! I fully expected to see Ottery St Mary on the national news tomorrow!"

"It still may be. They do report on happy news occasionally!"

"Can we see what going's on, now?" asked Ella.

"Certainly, follow me. Oh, by the way, my name's Judy. Trust my husband not to introduce us properly."

"Hello, Judy. I'm Ella and this is Frank, my husband."

"Welcome to our home!" laughed Judy.

She led them upstairs into the back bedroom from where they could clearly see the field with the grounded plane. Both wings had suffered severe damage. There was a hole in the front of the fuselage. One of the engines had detached itself from the wing and lay on the grass, its propeller arms bent at a strange angle. Vehicles and appliances were all scattered along one edge of the field near the footpath that followed the line of the old railway. Fire hoses snaked across the grass towards the plane. The fire brigade had covered both plane's engines with white foam. As they watched, a coach with Flybe markings on its side arrived. About thirty passengers and crew made their way towards it. Suddenly all the passengers stopped walking and formed a human corridor for one particular person. They were clapping and cheering as he walked towards the coach.

"I bet that's the pilot. He saved their lives!" said Geoff.

They watched for a while longer as the coach drove away across the grass and engineers and workmen gathered on and around the stricken aircraft. Local television crews arrived and began filming for the evening's regional news.

Frank turned to Ella, "Puts our little dip in the water into context. It was only a few feet deep, so we were in no real danger."

"Unlike the passengers in that plane. What happened to the engines? They went quiet all of a sudden. Could both engines just stop together–just like that?"

"I remember reading about something like that happening when I was younger. In that case, the fuel indicators were faulty. No-one had checked them and the plane simply ran out of fuel."

"I bet that's what happened here. It must have run out of fuel."

They went back downstairs, and Frank saw the envelope, still wrapped in plastic, lying on the small table by the sofa.

"Yet again, we've forgotten our treasure hunt. Open it up and let's see if Geoff can help us again!"

Ella unwrapped the envelope and extracted the green scalloped paper.

She read its contents out loud: *"The ringers go there every June, the parlour hides another clue."*

Judy clapped her hands in delighted discovery. "That's obvious!"

"Oh good," remarked Frank, "I've not a clue what it means!"

"I help with the Ottery Brownies. Pixies Parlour. That's the place where the pixies banish the bell ringers. It happens in June on Pixie Day."

"Where is Pixie's Parlour?" asked Ella.

"Not too far from here," said Geoff. "On the other side of the river where the plane landed."

"I'll see if Brown Owl can help you," Judy volunteered.

"Brown Owl? Who's Brown Owl?" asked Frank.

"Alice."

Ella suddenly felt at ease about this clue. "Don't tell me, Alice Aylesbeare?"

"Yes, how did you know her name?"

"Oh, it seems everyone knows Alice!"

~~~

Frank and Ella were back home in the warm and dry of their own home. As they supposed, the plane crash was not only featured on the regional TV news, but the national news also ran a short snippet at the end. The plane had, according to a reporter, allegedly run out of fuel. The reporter surmised that it may be because of faulty fuel gauges. The plane, a Flybe Dash 8, looked like a write-off but all of the twenty-eight passengers and five crew were able to walk away from the crash thanks to the cool-headed and skilful work of the pilot. Every passenger who was interviewed thanked him and praised his efforts. He was a hero in all their eyes.

It seems the only injuries occurred to two cows who collided with each other as they ran away from the approaching aircraft.

"Hope the cows are OK," pondered Ella.

"I'm glad the humans are safe. What a brilliant pilot. Someone's gonna be in a lot of trouble if those fuel gauges were faulty. They should have been checked."

The news programmes finished, and they switched off the TV and sat in companionable silence.

"We ought to give Alice a ring and see if she can help us," said Ella.

"Not just yet. I keep thinking about how close the people came to disaster.

☙❧

For the next few days, the sole topic of conversation in and around the Otter Valley was the plane crash. In Otterbury neighbours nattered over the garden fence chewing over every aspect of the near tragedy.

The pilot became a hero of the highest order.

"Someone should knight him."

"Or, at the very least, give him the freedom of the town."

Ottery became the centre of media attention. Visitors from around the locality came to gawk at the plane and marvel at how it had managed to land safely in a meadow beside the River Otter.

Frank and Ella kept a low profile. They did not want any journalist picking up the story of the Ottery Lottery or the subsequent death of Caleb Kennaway. They felt if they avoided going into Ottery then they would not be tempting fate.

༺༻

A week after the crash, the media had moved on to another story and Frank and Ella finally felt up to continuing the treasure hunt.

"Why don't we give Alice a ring today and see if she can help us," said Ella.

"No sooner said than done," replied Frank as he found her number on his mobile phone.

Alice answered straightaway. Frank explained the predicament.

"I'd love to help. Are you free tomorrow?"

Ella could hear Alice's question. She nodded.

"We most certainly are!"

"Good. Meet me by St Saviour's Bridge tomorrow morning at ten o'clock. Oh, by the way, wear walking boots and suitable clothing. We're going hiking!"

༺༻

Another balmy sunny Devon morning found Frank and Ella parked in the Canaan Way car park, changed into their walking boots and strolling down to St Saviour's Bridge. As they walked along Mill Street, they saw Alice in front of them.

Ella shouted, "Yoo-hoo, Alice!"

Alice stopped and waited for them to catch her up.

"Good morning, you two. How's the treasure hunt going?"

"You know very well. That's why you're here!" replied Ella.

"I know, just kidding. We're off to Pixie's Parlour. Do you know the story?"

"No, we're hoping you'd tell us."

"Well, every June on the Saturday nearest to Midsummer's Day, the good people of Ottery celebrate the banishing of the pixies from the town. They call it Pixies Day. The pixies were sent to the Pixies Parlour."

"Which is where we'll find the barrel or another clue?" added Frank.

"Tell us more about these pixies," asked Ella.

"I'll tell you as we go. Before we cross the bridge there's a path that leads to the river. We'll take the path –here it is."

They walked down alongside the river and passed by the footbridge.

"We're staying on the east bank. That's the Millennium Bridge."

"Built in 2000?" asked Frank.

"Of course."

They walked up through the woods.

"Now the story goes that when Bishop Grandisson built the church he commissioned some iron bells from Wales. Monks were sent to bring the bells back to Ottery. The pixies were worried that the sound of the bells would be the end for them, so they cast a spell over the monks."

"And the monks took the bells to Pixies Parlour?"

"No, the pixies redirected the monks to take the bells to Sidmouth and throw them over the cliffs and into the sea."

"Don't talk to me about Sidmouth cliffs," shuddered Ella.

"Don't worry. As they were heading there, one of the monks stubbed his toe and shouted out 'God, bless my soul!' and that broke the spell."

"And were the bells installed?"

"Yes. However, the spell was not completely broken because each year a pixie came out and captured the bell ringers and put them in Pixies Parlour."

"Who rescued them?" asked Ella.

"The vicar of Ottery St Mary! And that's why we have Pixies Day."

"What a quaint legend!" said Frank.

"Who's to say it isn't true?"

"So, Pixie Day goes back to medieval times?"

"Well, no, actually. It seems that in 1954 Ronnie Delderfield wrote…"

"Not RF Delderfield?" blurted Ella. "The one who wrote *'To Serve Them All My Days'* and *'A Horseman Riding By'*?"

"The very same. He lived in East Devon and worked on the local newspaper before he was a proper writer. Anyway, he wrote a pamphlet in 1954 about the pixies' revenge."

"Do you mean he invented the legend?"

"Well, to date, no-one's found any evidence about Pixies Day before 1954!"

"It's one of those invented traditions!" chuckled Frank.

"Anyway, here we are."

The three of them were stood in front of a small cave about four foot in height and about six foot across.

"I was expecting some kind of a house or old building, not a cave!"

Alice smiled. "I suppose in medieval times this was the height of luxury for pixies!"

Frank shrugged his shoulders. "What was the clue again?"

Ella took the envelope out of her pocket. She read: "*The ringers go there every June, the parlour hides another clue.*"

"The ringers are the bell ringers and the parlour is this cave, right here!"

Alice and Ella looked at the dusty entrance and turned to Frank.

"We need a brave knight to go in and explore the dragon's lair!"

"All right. I'll play the role! Reluctantly!"

Frank went down on his hands and knees and crawled into the cave. "It's dark. Hold on, I'm going to turn on my phone's flashlight."

There was a fifteen-second silence.

"Are you OK, Frank?"

"It's here!"

"Well done, my hero!" cheered Ella.

"But unfortunately, my lady, it's another envelope!"

He brought out the package. It was indeed, another envelope wrapped in a plastic bag.

"Open it," jabbered Alice impatiently.

Ella tore the plastic apart and extracted the envelope. Inside was another green scalloped sheet of paper.

"What does it say?" requested Alice.

"The curly haired female pew hides a misery called a clue."

"Misery is the right word," Frank hissed. "I'm getting a bit fed up with this. Another clue!"

"Are we going to sit down here and solve this?" appealed Alice.

"No. Sometimes a cup of tea or coffee gets the brain working better! We'll wait till we get home."

"Right," said Alice, "If you want to, we can carry on this walk."

"Yes, it's a perfect day for a walk."

"If you've got the time? We've got our boots on."

"I was hoping you would agree. It's a lovely walk up to Tipton St John and then back along the river to Ottery."

They left the Pixies Parlour and the River Otter behind and made their way through a gate in the fence and followed the hedge up to the road passing a lake on their left.

"That's Knightstone Lake. It's man-made and probably built in medieval times to provide fish for the Knightstone Manor."

"They did that quite a lot, didn't they?" said Frank. "Almost like the fisheries of today."

They crossed over the Sidmouth road and about one hundred and fifty-yards later turned right at a way-mark up into a field.

"Knightstone Manor's behind us. It's a private house now and used to be owned by the Marchioness of Dorset. She provided the money for the Dorset Aisle in the church when that was added in 1520."

"You're quite a hive of knowledge!" said an envious Frank.

"Not really. We're following the Coleridge Link for some of the route and I just read all this from one of their leaflets!"

"You're a bit like Frank! He's always trying to convince me he's the fount of all knowledge when most of the time he's just reading from pages he found on goggle!"

"Excuse me, you've been known to do exactly the same!" retorted Frank.

The good-humoured banter continued as they reached the lane leading down to Wiggaton.

"Turn right here," commanded Alice.

Ella saluted and obeyed.

However, before they reached the small village of Wiggaton, they turned up another footpath that led them along two sides of a square back to the Sidmouth road.

"You know, a couple of years ago, we could have just followed the river to Tipton and then crossed the bridge and followed the river back to Ottery."

"What happened?"

"Floods damaged the footpath so much that's it's unsafe in quite a few places."

Before they reached the road, they turned sharp left up another footpath and followed it past some farm buildings.

"This is a real zig-zag route, but it keeps us off the main road."

"I assume the Sidmouth road has no pavements for pedestrians?" mused Ella.

"Absolutely," replied Alice. "That road's dangerous enough for cars, let alone walkers!"

"Look out for a path on the right," Alice said. "It's called Lancercombe Lane and it leads back down again to the Sidmouth road."

They turned left down Lancercombe Lane.

Reaching the road, they carefully crossed and made their way down through a grassy field to the River Otter. Here the path was muddy but walkable with care.

"Up ahead is Tipton Mill. It goes back to Tudor times," informed Alice. "There's a bridge there across the river. We can cross it and follow the river back to Ottery."

"Just in time for a late lunch," muttered Frank.

"More like afternoon tea!"

They reached some factory buildings and turned right past the mill to the bridge.

"Wow! Look at that!" declared Ella.

"That is an Archimedes Screw." This time Frank was the provider of information. "It provides power for the mill. It used to be a flour mill but now this place is used to produce animal feed."

They crossed the bridge and spent some minutes staring at the Archimedes Screw. It was a giant screw placed within a concrete downhill shute. The screw rotated as the water flowed through its blade.

"It isn't always working," said Alice.

"It is today. It makes a bit of a clunking sound!" remarked Ella.

"But it's providing clean energy to the mill."

They continued following the river upstream and within a couple of hundred yards came upon another concrete construction.

"Tipton Mill Weir," announced Alice.

"It's a bit bigger than the Tumbling Weir in Ottery."

"Newer too. They let some of the river water continue down the river whilst some of it travels along that leat to the mill."

"That where the water to drive the Screw comes from!" cried Ella over the hub-bub of the water.

"Exactly."

"Those stones are massive."

"They had to be to stop the water eroding the dam!"

Yet again they spent some time enjoying the noisy spectacle of the water making its way through the dam. There was even a little diversion channel to the edge of the dam.

"Is that a salmon run?" asked Frank.

"I don't really know," replied Alice, "It certainly looks like it. Are there salmon around here?"

"Only in the shops!"

೭⊱⊰೨

They set off again following the river as it meandered through the flat floodplain. They passed the site of the crashed plane. Engineers and workmen were still swarming around it.

"I wonder if they'll cut it up to move it?" Ella pondered.

"They'll need a huge lorry, otherwise!" Alice smiled.

All too soon they were back at St Saviour's Bridge and Frank and Ella invited Alice to afternoon tea at their favourite cafe in the middle of Ottery.

Their boots were not too muddy, so they tramped into the cafe and found a table near the window before ordering a large pot of tea and a selection of cakes.

Frank saw the lady behind the counter nudging her husband as he prepared the tea tray.

"It's those two again!" she whispered. Discretion was not one of her superpowers.

"She's the one who won the Lottery," she continued.

The husband looked up and smiled. "Good afternoon, Brown Owl."

His wife carried on whispering. "Wonder what she wants?"

Alice interrupted them. "A cup of tea would be a good start!"

Tea and cakes were brought over to the table near the window and conversation ceased for a few minutes. Ella and Alice then discussed their Budleigh adventures and Alice's work as a Brown Owl. Frank asked for a piece of paper with the eighth clue.

"The curly-haired female pew hides a misery called a clue."

Both Ella and Alice turned towards him.

"They have pews in a church," offered Alice.

"Ottery's church again?" proposed Ella.

"Well, when you've finished your reminiscences, we could take a stroll up to the church."

"Not me, I'm afraid. I've got to pop home to turn myself into Brown Owl. I've got a pack meeting this evening."

"Oh, needs must. It's been a lovely day. You've helped us solve another clue and the walk was excellent. It was one of those we've never walked before."

"But we shall walk it again!" voiced Ella.

⊷⊶

They finished their tea and cakes and conversation. Frank and Ella made their way once more up to the church of St Mary's. This time the doors were firmly locked, and the push button didn't respond. They were unable to get in. Frank shrugged his shoulders.

"Oh well, back to the car. We'll try again tomorrow."

They turned around towards Silver Street only to see Carl Cooper walking towards them. He looked glum and despondent.

"Hello," said Ella, "Are you OK?"

Carl was suddenly shaken out of his reverie.

"Oh, it's you two. Haven't you heard the news?"

"About the crashed plane?"

"No, about Kenneth Kennaway."

"What's he done now?"

"He's dead!"

Chapter Thirteen

And all who heard should see them there,,/span>
And all should cry, Beware! Beware!

Frank and Ella stood there at the foot of Silver Street staring at Carl Cooper. They weren't sure how to reply to him.

"Are you sure? Last time we thought he died, he scooted off to Albania," Frank commented.

"There's where he died. In Albania," exclaimed Carl.

"Do you know how he died?" queried Ella.

"All I heard was that he was dead. That's all!"

"Wow, that's a great shock. Do you think that he killed Caleb?" Frank was more than a little concerned with this turn of events.

"Well, it certainly seems that way," continued Carl. "Perhaps we'll know more when the Albanian police reports are released."

"Yes, perhaps."

Frank and Ella walked through the centre of the town back towards the car park. Carl tagged alongside them as if he had something more to say.

"Oh, by the way," Carl turned to Ella, "I wanted to talk to you about the business."

"Kennaway Coopers?"

"Yes. Are you the official owner yet? Christine won't answer any of my questions."

"No, not yet," said Ella hesitantly. "Any day, I hope."

"Well, I'd like to make you an offer for the company when it's yours."

Ella chose her words carefully. "O.K, I'm interested. What did you have in mind?"

"I'll make you a decent offer for the whole business." Carl quickly explained, "I've got some backing. I can make it happen!"

"I'm interested, very interested." She felt she wanted to know more about Carl's motives. "What are you thinking of doing with the company?"

"Well, between you and me," Carl confided, "I think the premises are past their prime. It's time the company moved away from this town. I think there's a huge market that we're ignoring. Beer barrels, cider and wine caskets. There are plenty of breweries and vineyards looking for quality products. Kennaway Coopers can supply them."

Carl Cooper had become far more excited and enthusiastic than either Frank or Ella had ever seen him before.

"What about the tar barrels?"

"Oh, we won't need those anymore. They're going to close down the Tar Barrel Night soon anyway." Frank and Ella stopped walking, and both turned to him in genuine shock.

"But it's a wonderful quirky tradition," stammered Ella.

"No, it's not," replied Carl abruptly. "It's a dangerous, badly organised event. It's only a matter of time before someone dies. It's a health and safety nightmare. I should know!"

"Why?" asked Frank.

"Well…" Carl noticeably puffed out his chest and with unmistakable pride in his voice, continued, "I happen to serve on the Council's Health and Safety committee. I've almost persuaded enough members to vote for a health and safety close-down of the event."

"That's outrageous!" spluttered Frank, struggling to keep his voice down.

"No, it's just plain old common sense," maintained Carl. "When we submit our report to the full council, the papers will get hold of it. When the insurance companies see the report, they'll hike up their prices and the event will simply be unable to afford to continue."

"You've got it all planned, haven't you?" Frank was trying with decreasing success, to remain calm. "Does Christine Kennaway know about your plans?"

"That horrible woman? She never gives me the time of day in all our board meetings. Sometimes, I think, it's a waste of time for me to even attend. It's about time someone gave her a taste of her own medicine."

"But," countered Ella, "Christine doesn't have any control of the company. It's about to become mine and you're telling me you're going to try to take away my chief avenue of income."

"That's why I'm offering to buy it from you." Carl seemed oblivious to the rising antagonism from Ella and Frank.

Frank backtracked: "You said you'd move premises? Where?"

"Oh, I have up a deal with some lovely people up near Taunton."

"Not Taunton Norton?" asked Frank.

"Yes, do you know them?"

Ella chortled: "Yes, we've both heard of them?"

"Well, do I put a formal offer to you when you take over, Mrs Raleigh?" asked Carl.

Ella spun on her heels and began walking away back to their car. "I'm afraid, Mr Cooper," she said with a dismissive shake of her head, "the only phrase I can think of is–not in a million years."

Carl stood there confused. "Oh, is that a no, then?"

Without turning around, Ella raised her voice: "An absolute, unequivocal, unconditional, out and out....NO!" She continued walking towards the car.

Frank smiled, doffed an imaginary cap, and followed.

જેન્જી

"The cheek of the man," muttered Ella when Frank caught her up, "Closing down the company and moving it out of the county!"

"I think you made him very aware of your intentions!" replied Frank with a sympathetic smile.

They reached the car park to find Fabian Fassbender standing by their car.

"What do you want, Mr Fassbender?" asked Frank.

"I'd like to speak to Mrs Raleigh." Fabian stood up straight and bowed slightly to Ella.

Frank had still not completely calmed down from the conversation with Carl. "Well, make it quick, we're late for a meeting."

"Right, I will come straight to the point." His German accent was more pronounced than normal, "I wish to buy Kennaway Coopers from you when you take control."

"No," said Ella firmly.

Fabian staggered theatrically backwards in dismay. "But you have not heard my offer?"

Frank took the lead in this conversation. "Don't tell me, let me guess. You're going into partnership with Taunton Norton. You will be setting up a company in new premises and expanding your products? The local workforce will either have to come to Somerset or will simply be sacked. Am I right?"

"Where did you get his information from? It is most secret."

"But is it true?" Frank asked.

"Yes. My German backers are convinced it is a most viable solution."

Ella stepped in front of Fabian and pointed a finger towards him. "Then the answer is an absolute, unequivocal, unconditional, out and out....NO!"

Fabian spent a few seconds digesting the pronouncement before replying. "We will speak again."

"Not about this matter. Good afternoon!"

Ella opened the driver's side door of the car and got in.

Frank smiled, doffed another imaginary cap, and got in the passenger's side.

☙❧

"Where is this meeting that we're late for?" asked Ella when they had left Ottery and were heading for home.

"It's at our house around the dining table. It goes by the name of our evening meal!"

"That's one meeting we'll never be late for!" laughed Ella.

At home, they enjoyed their evening meal and then sat down in the living room to review progress.

"How many clues have we solved now?"

"I make it seven. But I do think the answer to the next clue is back in the parish church."

"Shall I read the clue out again?"

"Good idea!"

Ella reached into her handbag and pulled out the envelope with the clue inside it.

"How do you know which clue is which?" asked Frank.

"I only keep one clue at a time. I've put the rest in the drawer by the telephone. Now, this clue is number eight and it reads: *The curly-haired female pew hides a misery called a clue.*"

Ella stared at the words without any sign of comprehension. "A misery called a clue. A misery called… a clue?"

"Wait a moment," said Frank, "I was reading about the church the other day. Besides the clock, they talk about the misericords."

"Misery called? Same pronunciation just different words." Ella remarked with some satisfaction.

"Exactly."

"But what is a misericord?"

"Hold on a moment. Wikipedia is coming to the rescue!" Frank tapped a few words into his iPad and Wikipedia soon emerged.

Frank read from the page entry. "A misericord was sometimes called the mercy seat. Misericord means pity of the heart. When prayers were being said in medieval times, people were required to stand up. If the prayers went on a long time this became uncomfortable. So, someone made seating that could be turned up like a flip-up seat in a theatre. A shelf was carved on the underside of the seat to make it comfortable to lean against. The carving became very ornate even though it was hidden underneath the seat."

"And Ottery has got these misericords?"

Frank conducted another quick search and soon declared "Yes! Here's a website all about misericords!"

"Don't tell me, misericords.co.uk?"

Frank nodded and then read a bit in silence before paraphrasing. "The misericords were put in when the church was built in 1342 by John Grandisson. A number of them have got his coat of arms carved into the seat and one has…"

"The figure of a curly-haired female?"

"Exactly."

"Therefore, the next clue will be attached to the underneath of this seat?"

"I bet you a Devon Cream Tea it is."

"Hold on," Ella wanted to clarify the bet. "Does that mean if the clue is there you buy the cream tea and if it isn't, I buy it?"

"Yes."

"Well, seeing what's mine is your's and what's your's is mine, it's a win-win situation! A racing certainty!"

Frank put his iPad down on the sofa and went to make them both a cup of tea. When he returned, they moved onto Caleb Kennaway's death.

"We missed a great opportunity to question those two wheeler-dealers this afternoon," said Frank.

"Let's contact them again and meet up with them together and delve into their alibis."

"Yes," mused Frank, "I don't quite believe their stories- there's more to it than meets the eye."

"It's a pity there were no CCTV cameras around Kennaway House."

"True," agreed Frank, "Either Carl and Fabian could have come back."

"Or both. It's all a bit confusing at the moment. We need to pin down the time-line."

"Who was where and when?"

"And maybe even–why!" Ella added.

They thought in silence for a few minutes whilst sipping their tea.

"Do you think Kenneth killed him?" asked Ella.

"If he did, then it's a good chance it was manslaughter."

"And is he really dead?" wondered Ella.

Frank shook his head. "Somehow I don't believe it. He faked his death once– why not again?"

"But why again?"

Frank smiled. "Why? That's your word of the moment!" Ella grinned as Frank continued. "Something must have happened. Perhaps he thought someone wanted him to come back to England to face the police."

Ella nodded before another thought struck her. "Are you sure that the Zummerset Zyder gang couldn't have been involved?"

"I don't think so. They had too much to lose. No, I think it's down to one of those four who had the evening argument with Caleb."

Ella was on a roll. "Right then, what about Christine? She's got a temper. She must have been very angry. She's strong enough to push her husband through the bannisters."

"But is she capable, psychologically, of killing him?"

"Perhaps there is somebody else?" Ella stopped and tried to put her thoughts into coherent words. "Perhaps this is not about the company but it's about getting rid of the husband so she can get together with her lover?"

Frank shook his head. "That's a bit convoluted. Before we head down that avenue, I think we should ask if anyone's heard rumours about any liaisons!" Frank sat there thinking things through. "We definitely need to speak to our wheeler–dealers but how do we contact them?"

"Surely Elsie or Alf will be able to help us?" said Ella.

"I'll give them a call in the morning." Frank changed the subject. "Now, what about Kennaway Coopers? We need to visit the company and talk with some of the workers about their future."

"Before we actually own the place?" asked Ella.

"Yes. You can go on your own if you want, or I can come with you."

Ella got up from her armchair and stepped towards Frank. "Let's get one thing clear. *If* Kennaway Coopers ever becomes *ours*, then it is *ours*, not mine. It may be my name on the lottery ticket, but we share."

She sat down on Frank's lap. "We're in this together whether it's solving crimes or running companies." She leaned down to kiss him. "And don't you forget it!"

꙳

Sergeant Elsie Knowle answered her phone and was pleased to hear Frank's voice.

"Hello, Frank. If you've called to ask about Kenneth Kennaway, I've heard nothing from the Albanian police force."

"Do you think it's another faked death?"

"It wouldn't surprise me. But if it is, then he's going the right way to attract our interest. Why does he want us to believe he's dead?"

"Because he thinks we think he killed Caleb," countered Frank.

"Exactly. And who's to say he didn't?"

"That's not the reason I called. We bumped into both Carl Cooper and Fabian Fassbender yesterday and it's left us with the feeling that we need to have a proper chat with them."

"Do I need to arrest them?"

"No, I don't think so. Can you give us their phone numbers so I can contact them and set up a meeting?"

"No. That's private information. GDPR and all that!"

"Oh. Perhaps I can contact the company and see if they'll tell me."

"They won't if they understand the law. However, I will set up a meeting for you. Mr Cooper and Mr Fassbender will be at the King's Inn tomorrow morning at eleven o'clock on the dot!"

"That's great. Thank you."

Elsie hadn't finished with the two directors yet. "I've got some information you might interesting. We've been laboriously checking the CCTV cameras at Cranbrook. Fabian did go home but he left once again about half an hour later."

"To go back to Kennaway Court?"

"I couldn't find any evidence of that. Ask him yourself, tomorrow."

"We will! Anything more about Carl Cooper?"

"No. He did go to his meeting and he did leave to go home at the time he said. His wife confirmed his arrival. She was waiting on the doorstep."

"Thanks!"

"How are you progressing with your treasure hunt? I hear you're following a trail of clues. Caleb obviously had a great sense of humour."

"We don't always find his sense of humour very funny. We've been all over Ottery. Now we're back at the church later on today searching for a misericord."

"You know, I think Caleb was a very astute person. Anyone willing to take on Kennaway Coopers needs grit and determination. They need to know the local area and show some commitment to the town. He's giving you the chance to do just that!"

"From beyond the grave!"

"If he's looking down on you, I don't think you'll disappoint him!"

"No, I think you're absolutely correct. Thanks!"

꙳

Later that morning Frank and Ella entered St Mary's Church in Ottery. This time the push-button device immediately opened the doors. On the far side of the church, three ladies were arranging flowers for the weekend's services. Each of them stopped and gestured greetings to the couple.

Ella smiled and went over to the nearest lady.

"Good morning. Excuse me, can you help us? We're looking for the misericords."

"Over there, m'dear," she said, pointing towards the altar, "Go behind the altar to the Lady Chapel. You'll see them there. Lift up the seats and look underneath."

"We're looking specifically for one that has a female head with curls on either side of her face."

"We haven't got *one*." She emphasised the last word. "We have, however, got *five* of them. Five females and five of Bishop Grandisson's coat of arms."

"Thanks, we'll go and look at them all!"

"Don't make no noise in there, mind. It be a place for quiet con‑tem‑plation."

She split the last word in the sentence into three distinct syllables.

Before they could continue, the church bells welcomed twelve o'clock midday. The three ladies waited for the bells to finish and then burst robustly into song!

> *"Sweet-breathing kine,*
> *The old grey Church,*
> *The curfew tolling slow,*
> *The glory of the Western Sky,*
> *The warm red earth below.*
> *O! Ottery dear! O! Ottery fair!*
> *My heart goes out to thee,*
> *Thou art my home, wher'er I roam,*
> *The West! The West for me!"*

Frank and Ella looked at each other. "What was all that about?" laughed Frank.

"That were the Ottery song," the nearest lady replied. "It's sung after the peal of the church bells and at the funeral of an Old Ottregian."

"Old Ottregian?"

"Yes, an inhabitant of Ottery St Mary."

"It's a stirring song," said Ella.

"Best in the West!" she said proudly.

"Thank you," said Frank, "we'll go and look for our misericords."

"*Floreat Ottregia!*" choralled one of the ladies as she picked up some carnations.

"Pardon?"

"*May Ottery Flourish*, the motto of the Old Ottregians Society."

The three ladies went back to their flower arranging.

"I think we've entered a parallel universe," whispered Frank as they walked past the altar.

They found the old wooden seats and looked underneath them, one by one. The seats had rounded wooden backs and were well varnished. The wood was a deep and ancient brown. They had discovered three of the female heads with no sign of a clue when on the fourth female Frank noticed a string attached to the seat. He pulled on it gently and an envelope appeared from underneath the back of the seat.

"Got it," he said as quietly as he could.

Ella took the envelope and opened it. "This will be clue number nine!"

Frank leaned towards Ella, keen to see the contents. "Green scalloped paper. It's the real deal! What does it say?"

"*Beside the kerb of Kubla Khan, a tree will shield a lucky charm!*"

"Yes," shouted Frank.

The three ladies stopped their flower arranging and turned to stare at him.

"Lovely carving," stumbled Frank. "Quite exquisite!" He felt himself going red in the face and wished the large gravestone slab that lay on the floor of the church below his feet would open up. Then he considered that would be too gruesome.

"Can we go now?" he asked Ella.

"Certainly!" She stood by the chair with the misericord and returned the chair seat to its horizontal position before turning back to Frank with a beam on her face. "Is it too hot in here for you?"

Ella bid the ladies farewell. "Sorry about that! Those flowers are just lovely. I love hydrangea flower-heads."

Outside the church, they stood on the tarmac path leading down to Silver Street. "Where next?" asked Ella.

"Home. Lunchtime."

Frank's phone buzzed.

"You've got a message."

Frank's fingers moved slowly around the screen until he'd found the message icon, opened it and clicked on the new message.

"Elsie wants me to give her a ring."

"It'll wait till we get home."

There were gusts of wind blowing in their faces as they walked down Silver Street and back to the car.

Ella gripped the envelope tightly and muttered: "This next clue is a breeze."

Chapter Fourteen

Be sad ! be glad ! be neither! seek, or shun!
Thou hast no reason why ! Thou canst have none;
Thy being's being is contradiction.

Frank was soon back on the phone to the police sergeant. He switched his phone to loudspeaker so that Ella could hear both sides of the conversation.

"Hi Frank, it's all been happening here this morning."

"Great. Fire away!"

"Kenneth contacted me. The Albanian police were waiting for him when he went for a meeting with Christine Kennaway's charity director."

"So, he's not dead. Again!" Frank was somehow not surprised.

"No, this attempt was quite pathetic."

"Why?"

"Well, the police received an anonymous phone call saying some British tourist had run off the road and crashed off a cliff into the sea near Ksamil, a village near Sarandë."

"That's where the charity is based, isn't it?"

"Yes. They went to search but, of course, found no body. Only an old push–bike with a battered pannier attached to the frame stuck halfway down the cliff. In it was an envelope with a rather compromising photo of the director of the charity with Christine.

With it was a note written to Christine Kennaway by the director declaring his undying love for her and how Kenneth would soon have a new stepfather. Then the police questioned a few witnesses who all said they saw a frantic young man tip the old bike over a crash barrier down the cliff and into the sea and then run away."

"And that young man was Kenneth?" asked Frank.

"Absolutely!" replied Elsie.

"Intriguing!" whispered Ella.

"The police contacted the director and he told them he had received a phone call from Kenneth asking him to meet him down by the beach that afternoon. The local policeman simply waited for Kenneth to arrive and arrested him."

"For stealing a push-bike?" Ella was quite concerned for the poor boy.

"And for wasting police time. The Ksamil policeman is a zero-tolerance type of man. He took him to the Sarandë police station. They gave Kenneth the phone number of a local ex-pat lawyer and allowed him his one phone call."

"But he phoned his mum instead?" guessed Frank.

"No, quite the opposite. He phoned me and pleaded with me not to contact his mum or anybody else. The Albanian police are sending him back to England this evening. I'm meeting with him the day after tomorrow in Exeter."

"Can we come along?" asked Ella.

"I don't see why not? It's not an official police interview. He's going to be staying at a local hotel and I'm going to see him there."

"Does he still think he killed Caleb?" wondered Ella.

"We didn't specifically discuss it, but I didn't offer any sort of an opinion on the matter."

"Do you think he might make another effort to disappear?" Frank was hoping for a negative answer.

"No, he sounded as if he was fed up with all the trouble he was in. He just wants to sort it out and face whatever comes his way!"

Frank smiled and Ella nodded. "Very mature," she said. "At last he may be growing up."

"I don't think you should mention any of this to Mr Cooper or Mr Fassbender when you meet them."

"We have no intention of telling *them* anything," replied Frank. "It's about time they told *us* the truth!"

༄

They met Carl and Fabian as planned. Frank and Ella sat in the King's Inn and were pleased to see the pair walk into the pub at exactly eleven o'clock. Ella surreptitiously switched on her phone's Dictaphone app and left the phone on the table. Frank waved them over to the table which had been carefully selected due to its position well away from any eavesdroppers.

"Morning," mumbled Carl. "I'm told by some police sergeant that you wanted to see us."

"Yes, Elsie said you'd be only too willing to have a pleasant conversation. We've ordered coffee. Unless you'd like something stronger?"

Both Fabian and Carl shook their heads. "No, coffee will be perfect," replied Fabian.

Ella smiled and was just about to speak when a youngish girl interrupted her with the coffees. "Here are your coffees. If you want refills, bring your cups over to the bar."

"Thank you!" offered Frank.

"Enjoy!" The youngish girl disappeared back towards what Frank assumed were the kitchens.

Ella passed the coffees around and Carl dropped three lumps of sugar into his cup.

"Now," started Frank, "I wanted to ask you why you lied to the police when we were last at Kennaway Court."

Carl looked incredulously at him, "But…."

"No, not you Carl. Fabian."

"I do not understand?" mumbled Fabian.

"You said you didn't return to Kennaway Court," continued Frank. "You even challenged Sergeant Knowle to check the cameras."

"And you won't see my car on any cameras between Cranbrook and Ottery!"

Frank nodded. "Not true. Maybe not on the route you usually take. But you did go back another way. Along the A30 and then passed Patteson's Cross. The cameras outside Otter Nursery picked you up at about an hour after you first left Kennaway Court."

"But...?" Fabian was stunned.

"Why did you go back?" asked Ella.

"It was not to kill him." Fabian's voice was reluctant but calm and Ella thought he was telling the truth. "I became concerned about Kenneth. He was extremely drunk. I left him downstairs finishing off another bottle when I first left."

"So, you did go back? You fool?" snarled Carl.

"It was not to kill him, I tell you. When I got there the front door was not locked. I just walked straight in." Fabian looked straight at Ella. His eyes silently begging her to believe him. "Kenneth was fast asleep face down in the same room downstairs. I shook him awake and helped him upstairs. He was just about aware enough for me to guide him to his room. I took off his shoes and laid him down on the bed with his head on top of three pillows so that he wouldn't drown if he vomited."

"Didn't anybody see you?" continued Frank.

"No. Looking back, it's a pity no one did. It could have saved a life."

"How do you mean?" asked Ella.

"Well, there was a very loud argument going on between two people in what I assumed was Caleb's bedroom."

Ella leaned forward. "Didn't you recognise the two people's voices?"

"I assumed it was Caleb and Christine. But they were shouting so loudly, and the language was so profane that I didn't dare interrupt."

"Could it have been Carl and Caleb?" asked Frank.

Carl stared daggers at Fabian.

Fabian shrugged his shoulders. "It could have been, but somehow, it didn't seem like the kind of language Carl would use. The other person was too forceful."

"Damned by faint praise," stuttered Carl.

"What was the argument about?" asked Ella.

"Well, it was hard to tell. I assumed it was a continuation of that evening's discussion. However, it was far more violent and aggressive, so I didn't hang around to hear anymore."

Frank saw the look in Fabian's eyes but couldn't decide whether he was being told the whole truth. "I find it hard to believe you went back just to check on Kenneth?" stated Frank.

"But it's the truth."

"Really?" Frank was still not convinced.

"Really. You see Kenneth confided in me about his problems." Fabian's voice became a little more desperate. "He told me his mother and father do nothing to help him. They don't believe in him. They had no intention of letting him take control of Kennaway Coopers."

"So? Why would you want to help him?" asked Ella.

"I need him on my side. When I heard of Caleb's plans, I contacted some business friends of mine in Bavaria. They are very interested in gaining a foothold in a successful barrel-making company here in England."

"A European takeover?" gasped Carl.

"You're a fine one to talk!" replied Fabian.

"We'll talk with you in a moment, Carl." Frank wanted to hear more from Fabian.

"I didn't want anything to happen to Kenneth. I felt that something wasn't quite right with him that evening. I phoned his mobile but got no reply, so I thought I'd better come back to check. I came back along the A30 because I could drive at a faster speed than my usual route."

Ella chipped in. "It appears, Fabian, that you have no alibi. You were in the house when Caleb died. No-one can corroborate your story. It could have been you who pushed him to his death."

"Yes, it could have been, but it wasn't." Fabian crossed his arms in a gesture of defiance.

Frank turned to Carl. "Why are you a 'fine one to talk'?"

"Because I, too, wanted to sell the company," confessed Carl.

"Yes, you made an offer for the company to me and then told me you were going to move it to Taunton." Ella was reminded of the outrageous suggestion.

"I can't deny that, because it's true. It's become so entangled with that horrible Tar Barrel Night. If the only way that I could shut down Tar Barrel Night, was to close the company, I wouldn't hesitate. But I'd much rather buy it from you and move it away."

"Why would you want to shut down such a lovely traditional event? Surely we want to keep our traditions?"

"Lovely? It's a health and safety nightmare. Have you ever been in the middle of the crowd when the tar barrels come by you? It's a wonder no-one's been burnt, maimed or killed. We need to replace the event with something safer, something more controlled."

"Was that the meeting you went to attend?"

"Yes. We are very close to persuading some very important people to investigate a safer Tar Barrel night. We could use plastic barrels with maybe, a hologram of a flame. We could keep the crowds back onto the pavements and put up barriers to protect them. We could limit the amount of alcohol sold, limit the crowds and make the bonfire smaller. There's so many things we could do to make it safer for our townsfolk and our visitors."

"Sounds rather boring to me," concluded Ella.

Carl huffed. "Better to be boring than to be dead!"

"Surely, your way of running Tar Barrel Night wouldn't attract so many visitors," asked Frank. Somehow the conversation had moved away from Fabian and onto Carl. "In fact, it could lead to the end of Tar Barrel Night in a few years."

"If it keeps the people of Ottery safe, then so be it!"

"That would ruin Kennaway Coopers," said Fabian.

"Not if you've already sold it!"

"Let's go back to the evening of Caleb's death, can we?" asked Frank. "You say you went to a meeting that finished at half-past ten and that you were home in bed by eleven o'clock?"

"Correct?"

"You live in Ottery, so you could have walked home via Kennaway Court. It could have been your voice that Fabian heard. You could have pushed Caleb to his death," stated Frank.

"I could, but I didn't. Now, twice I've been interrogated and each time I've told the truth. I have nothing to hide." Carl was not as controlled as Fabian. There was sweat on his forehead and he didn't quite know what to do with his hands. "You know what I think about Tar Barrel Night. I may be guilty of indirectly trying to ruin Caleb's company, but I did not kill him!"

Carl drank up his coffee, wiped his mouth and forehead with a serviette and smiled wanly at Frank and Ella. "Now, unless you have any firm evidence linking me with Caleb's death, then I suggest you let me get on with my poor excuse for a life."

Carl got up from his chair and left. Fabian soon followed.

"If I didn't know you better, I would say that that was a bit of a waste of time," said Ella.

"But you do know me. Too well!" Frank countered. "I think it's becoming very obvious who killed Caleb Kennaway."

❧

Elsie Knowle phoned to let Frank and Ella know that Kenneth was back in the country and ready to talk. "He's very happy to speak to both of you. He wants to apologise for his stalking behaviour."

They met up at a small country-style hotel on the outskirts of Exeter. They all sat by the French windows in the sunny guest lounge. They were the only people in the room. Kenneth was drinking water leaving the rest to do battle with a large pot of tea and some Devon cream cakes.

"Welcome home, Kenneth," greeted Ella with a cheerful smile.

"It's good to be home." Kenneth looked relieved. "I feel I've let a few people down, including you two. It's time to stand up and be counted."

Frank told both Elsie and Kenneth about the conversations they had with both Carl and Fabian.

"Fabian's always looked out for me. I believe his account of his return to Kennaway House."

"Do you think he killed your father?" asked Ella.

"No, I don't think I do."

Frank smiled. "What about Carl?"

"He's an old stick in the mud," grinned Kenneth. "I thought he was too scared of his own shadow but perhaps he's got more about him. He must know that he'd be very unpopular with the whole town if he pursued this vendetta against the Tar Barrels."

"Yet he's prepared to go through with it?" added Elsie.

"Indeed!" ruminated Frank.

"What about your mum?" asked Ella.

"She's got a vile temper. She used to smack me quite hard when I was younger. Even into my teens, she could have me cowering in a corner. Dad normally kept her under control–but now, I don't know?"

Elsie changed the subject. "Tell Frank and Ella about your trip to Albania."

"I chose Albania because of the holidays we had in nearby Greece. We used to go to Corfu and where we stayed you could see the mainland of Albania. It was only a few miles away. Mum and Dad told me tales of the old communist regime and how they were effectively kicked out in the nineties."

Kenneth took a sip of his water and looked out of the French windows with a smile on his face.

"One day we hired a motorboat and for an adventure crossed the sea to Albania. We weren't challenged. In fact, we were welcomed. After that day, we went across regularly. We walked to a small seaside village called Ksamil and discovered a small ramshackle orphanage. It was a relic from the communist era. We got to know the workers and the director, Besart Clifteli. When we came home, Mum wrote to him and asked if we could help in any way."

A small frown appeared on his face.

"The next year, Mum and I went back to Corfu. I think Dad was too busy with work or something. We spent more and more time at the orphanage. Mum took lots of pictures and spent hours discussing plans with the director. I joined some of the children down on the beach showing them how to build sandcastles and teaching them a few words of English."

"And the charity?" asked Frank.

"Mum set it up the next year. We raised a lot of money here in England and, to be honest, we made a big difference to those children's lives."

"Well done!" beamed Ella.

"Thanks. The next few years Mum took some of her holidays in Ksamil. She always came back looking so happy. Last week I found out why!"

"You visited the charity and met the director?" questioned Elsie.

"Yes, I escaped Dad's death by flying to Tirana. I hitch-hiked down to Sarandë and then on to Ksamil. I stayed with the director intending to spend my days working at the orphanage."

Ella stared at him. "What went wrong?"

☙❧

"What are you doing in my study, Kenneth?"

"This picture, Besart. That's you and my mum. That's disgusting. Why do you keep a picture like that for anyone to see?"

"This is my private study. No-one comes in here. Anyway, what is wrong with a picture of two people so happy and in love?"

"No wonder she returned home looking happier than when she left. You are her lover?"

"Of course. And one day soon, her husband."

"What do you mean?"

"I hear about your father's death. She rings me to tell."

"I thought she was helping to run the charity?"

"She is. But sometimes love becomes more important than work. Anyway, don't worry. Soon you will have another father. Me!"

"Aren't you sorry about Dad's death? You don't sound sorry!"

"I am pleased that your mother and myself can be together, at long last. You can join us. We will be one happy family."

"I don't think so. Not in a million years."

"Then I suggest you go back to your Devon home."

"That's not possible. I don't think I'm very welcome there at the moment."

"If you are so opposed to your mother and myself getting married then you are not welcome here either. Here, before you go, take this photo and my latest letter. I will put it in an envelope. You can deliver it to your mother personally!"

※

"He seems like a nice man?" said Elsie in a disparaging voice.

"Nice, he was horrendous. Oh, I see, sorry. You were being…"

"Sarcastic. No, I'm sorry," apologised Elsie, "It was an unhelpful comment. Please go on."

"It was out of the frying pan and into the fire! I couldn't believe it. I took an old bike I saw lying around and went off for a ride. I took the envelope with me intending to throw it off a cliff into the Ionian Sea. I had no intention of being a go-between. I was so angry. My mind was whirring. I couldn't think straight. I stopped at the top of on this hilly road. I was out of breath."

※

"Wow. What a view down there!

I could just fly away!

Just get on the bike and cycle over the edge.

No-one would care. There's no-one around.

No. I know. I've got a better idea. I'll push the bike over. Leave the envelope in it. Someone will find it and think I drowned in the sea.

Even better. I'll meet up with this director sleaze down by the beach. Hire a boat, take a trip towards Corfu and push him overboard.

It makes little difference to me if I'm convicted for one or two murders.

Make sure the envelope stays in the pannier basket.

Give it a good hearty push.

I feel like I've done this before!

There it goes. Now I need to get away from the scene of this tragic death as soon as possible.

❧❦

Kenneth continued his story. "I met up with Sleazebag on the beach. I told him my thoughts about my father's death. I told him it was murder. He looked shocked. That's when the policeman arrived. Sleazebag, sorry, Besart Clifteli, had phoned him as soon as he saw me arrive. The policeman was almost as big as your PC Hydon. He escorted me to jail in Sarandë where I managed to persuade them to let me have one phone call. I phoned you and here I am. The Albanian police never told sleazebag that they set me free. He thinks I'm in jail in Sarandë. He'll tell Mum if he knows. I don't want mum to know I'm here."

"I've been thinking things through all the way home. The fewer people who know I'm here, the better. I'm certain I know who the murderer is, and I want them caught."

Chapter Fifteen

And there were gardens bright with sinuous rills,
Where blossomed many an incense-bearing tree;

Frank and Ella sat at home wondering what to do next?

"Do we invite Elsie and Alf around and sort out how to confront the murderer?"

"Or do we solve this treasure hunt?" mused Frank.

"I think we have a better chance of forcing the murderer's hand if we owned the company."

"You mean, a position of power, rattling the cage of a trapped predator?"

"Exactly!"

"Well, let's do it, then," said Frank. "What was the ninth clue?"

"Beside the kerb of Kubla Khan, A tree will shield a lucky charm."

"And if I remember you said you'd already solved it."

"Yes, it has to be the Samuel Taylor Coleridge Poetry Stones that we saw. The poem was Kubla Khan. There'll be a tree nearby! And in that tree, they'll be a clue or a miniature beer barrel."

"Let's go and see if you're correct!"

They parked and walked down the pathway alongside the Poetry Stones. As Ella had remembered, the poem was Kubla Khan. There were four trees alongside the granite stones. Frank and Ella searched in earnest but could find no envelope or beer barrel in any of the trees.

"I can't have got it wrong. *A tree will shield a lucky charm.*"

"Is there a tree in the poem?" asked Frank.

They went to the top of the path and read each stone.

"Eureka," cried Ella. She read out the writing on a stone *"Where blossomed many an incense-bearing tree; And here were forests ancient as the hills, Enfolding sunny spots of greenery."*

Frank bent down and picked up an ice lolly stick that someone had pushed into the earth alongside the stone.

"There's writing on this stick!"

"It'll be some silly joke," replied Ella. "They're always putting jokes on those sticks. I'll throw it away when we see a bin."

"No, no. This is not a joke. It's a clue."

Frank read out the words that had been written in tiny writing along both sides of the lolly.

> *"My pink has now transformed to blue*
> *Above the treasure's final clue."*

Ella looked around. "Where's the envelope? The scalloped paper?"

"There is no envelope or paper because this is the final clue!" Frank stood there in silent cogitation. "I think I've got it!" shouted Frank.

"Spill the beans!"

"When we were at Otter Nurseries, we saw lots of red hydrangeas and we couldn't find a blue one anywhere."

Ella nodded and then commented: "Aren't the colours of hydrangeas dependent on the soil in which they're planted?"

"You're right," said Frank.

"So, somewhere in Ottery someone has planted a pink hydrangea and it's now blue?"

"And the beer barrel is buried underneath the hydrangea."

Ella clapped her hands in delight before stopping. "Who can help us?" she reflected in a more despondent voice. "Do we have to dig up every blue hydrangea in Ottery?"

"No, we need to find someone who knows about the soil in this area."

Ella's face lit up once more. "Let's go back to the garden centre and speak to the manager. What was his name?"

"Harry Baker."

ஒ~ஒ

"Can we speak to Harry Baker, the manager please?" asked Ella.

The lady behind the customer services counter smiled at them both. "Certainly, can I ask what it's about?"

"Yes, we need to pick his brains about hydrangeas."

They were soon in Harry Baker's office.

"I remember you two. The treasure seekers. Are you still seeking, or have you given up?"

"No, we're on the last leg and we're hoping you can help us." Ella replied enthusiastically. "The last clue is about a pink hydrangea plant that has now turned to blue."

"Ah, that's because of the soil around here. It's loamy and slightly acidic. If you plant a pink hydrangea then there is a chance its blooms will change colour to blue."

"Do you sell many pink hydrangeas?" asked Frank.

"Hardly any. They're best in alkaline soil. We sell a ton of blue hydrangeas because gardeners get to know which ones will flourish in the East Devon soil."

"That's why we only saw pink and red hydrangeas the last time we were here," remarked Frank. "You'd sold out of the blue hydrangeas that we were looking for."

"Do we know if anyone local has bought any pink hydrangeas in the past year or so?" queried Ella.

"Why?"

"Because our clue says *"My pink has now transformed to blue above the treasure's final clue."*

"Therefore, I think, someone bought pink hydrangeas a while ago, planted them in the soil and now they've changed to blue! Do you know anyone?"

Harry Baker grinned at the impeccable logic. "No, but I know a lady who might be able to help you. Hold on, I'll call down for her."

He picked up his phone. "Bessie, darling, could you pop upstairs for a chat with our treasure seekers?"

"Bessie, darling?" mouthed Ella to Frank.

Harry read her lips. "Bessie is my wife. She works on the customer service counter."

Bessie Baker knocked on the door and came in.

"Bessie, dearest. Have we sold any pink hydrangeas to anyone in the last year or so?"

"Can I borrow your computer and I'll check my database?"

Harry moved out of the way and Bessie's fingers flew over the keyboard. In less than a minute she had come up with an answer.

"A couple of people from Ottery. One, an old dear who lives in the flats over at Yonder Close. She bought a couple of bushes for her son and his family for a Christmas present. However, they live in Australia. It would have cost her a fortune to send them. But she was very determined. She told me that you couldn't buy such great plants anywhere else in the world. Between you and me, we subsidised most of the postage cost ourselves. I think I might have fallen for her soft soap story!"

"Anyone else?" asked Ella sweetly.

"Just one more. One you'll recognise."

"Who?" asked Ella.

"Caleb Kennaway."

<hr />

Frank and Ella thanked the pair and made their way quickly back to their car.

"That means that somewhere in Caleb's garden at Kennaway Court is a recently planted hydrangea bush that has turned from pink to blue," stated Frank.

"And under it should be our beer barrel."

"Quite ironic that the deeds to the company have been right under the noses of the Kennaway family all this time."

"Do you think Christine and Kenneth know?" asked Ella

"I doubt it. There's one problem, though. We've got to get into Kennaway Court, search around the garden and dig up any hydrangea bush we find in the hope that the beer barrel is buried underneath!"

"There could be loads of bushes. Do we need a search warrant?"

Frank was deep in thought.

Ella knew better than to interrupt his thinking.

"Open afternoons. We were waiting in Kennaway Court for the result of the Ottery Lottery and some dear ladies near us were talking about Sunday afternoon openings."

Ella smiled. "Right, that's easy. We go with our spades and wander around digging up random blue hydrangeas?"

"No, I don't think so. But we can spend some profitable time checking out where the blue hydrangeas are, and which are worth checking out further."

❧❧

The next Sunday afternoon, Frank and Ella ambled down College Lane and into Kennaway Court's glorious gardens. Most of the gardens were laid out like parkland. The green luscious lawns flowed down to the River Otter. It created a gorgeous Sunday afternoon stroll. Back nearer the house, some ladies had set up a refreshment table. A dozen or so chairs were dotted around the table which was doing brisk business.

"First things first." Frank manoeuvred Ella away from the inviting Devon Cream teas.

"First before thirst!!"

They made for the shrubs and bushes which were laid in clusters around the edges of the parkland. Laurel bushes, rhododendrons, azaleas and many more that neither Frank nor Ella recognised. They found one old hydrangea hiding near a brick wall that was more purple than blue and was on its last legs.

"That one does not look young enough!"

"I bet its roots go way down, though."

They made their way around the kitchen garden and went through a walled gateway on the far side, well away from the house. They were now standing in a gravel area about the size of a small netball court. On the far side they could see a stone boundary wall signifying the edge of the Kennaway Court property. It was about five foot high and there growing up against it were a small group of red azaleas and youngish looking blue hydrangeas.

"Bingo!" whispered Ella.

"There's no need to whisper," replied Frank. "This seems to be sort of a hidden garden. Let's just stay here for a few minutes and see who comes this way."

Not one person made their way through the walled gateway. Frank and Ella explored the enclosed area examining each of the three hydrangeas bushes with interest. One looked more than a couple of years old. The bush on the end of the group had a lot of different textured soil and remnants of manure around it.

"This one looks promising," pronounced Frank. "Someone's spent some time cultivating this plant. Look at all the fertiliser that's been used."

"To increase the acidity?"

"Yes. This one could be the one."

"Can't you get down on your hands and knees and scrabble away now?"

"No, we'd look a bit obvious crossing the lawns with dirty hands carrying an earth encrusted beer barrel!" Ella smiled and understood his response.

Frank looked at Ella's weekend clothing. "We're not dressed or equipped for digging."

Yet again Ella silently agreed.

Frank was looking around the surroundings. "I think we could come back to this area with our spades and dig away without fear of being disturbed."

Ella studied the boundary wall. "We wouldn't even need to come in through College Lane," added Ella.

"You're right. Simply clamber over the boundary wall."

"Let's come back this evening armed with our spades."

They walked back through the Kitchen Garden. Again, they encountered no visitors. Everyone was either walking around the gardens, fixated by the gentle River Otter or enjoying their Devon Cream Tea.

Frank and Ella joined the cream tea brigade and spent the rest of the afternoon imagining themselves as part of a very select 1930's country house party taking high tea on the lawns and exchanging gentle gossip about recent local balls, galas and regattas.

ॐ

A completely different Frank and Ella reappeared at Kennaway Court in the late evening. Dressed in darker, work-ready clothes, they both wore gardening gloves and baseball caps pulled down to obscure their faces. Ella baulked at the idea of rubbing soil or boot polish into their faces for camouflage.

It was twilight as they parked as close to the boundary wall as they dared. Ella had brought along a two-step ladder from the kitchen. She placed it up against the wall and Frank clambered over with ease. Ella passed him the two spades which he dropped beside the bushes. He then offered a hand to Ella, but she declined any assistance and nimbly joined him in the Kennaway Court gardens bringing the ladder with her.

"Here's the one," said Frank in a quiet determined voice, "Are you ready to have your life changed?"

"Come on, get digging!"

They attacked the fertilised soil, one of each side of the bush. The roots were still reasonably shallow and within five minutes they had dug down a couple of feet. The bush swayed from side to side as Frank shifted it first one way and then the other. Ella was on her hands and knees grappling beneath the plant.

"There's something here!"

"Wow, first time! We found it first time!" Frank was amazed.

"Don't forget the ten clues it took to get here!"

Carefully Frank moved the hydrangea to one side and they each cautiously dug around the object. It was a box. A dirty, earth-covered, steel box. Certainly, big enough to contain something like a miniature beer barrel.

There were two handles on opposite sides of the box. Frank held onto one and Ella grabbed the other. With deceptive ease, they lifted the box clear of its hiding place before placing it onto the gravel area.

Ella clapped her hands together, then suddenly stopped and turned to Frank. "We have a problem."

"What problem. We've found this box. I bet you a month's worth of washing up that the beer barrel is inside it."

"You're right, I'm sure. But how do we get into it?"

"Well, we simply open the lid. Oh, I see."

Frank brushed away some of the earth and examined the lid of the box. He immediately found it was locked.

"Remember when we were in Kennaway Court the afternoon of the Ottery Lottery?"

"Yes?" answered Frank trying to follow where this conversation was going.

"We were handed an envelope. Inside the envelope were the letter and the first clue?"

"Yes?"

"There was something else in the envelope as well."

"Is this what you're looking for?"

The voice behind them made both of them jump.

Standing under the walled gateway, holding up a small, shiny metal key was Christine Kennaway.

Chapter Sixteen

*Henceforth I shall know
That Nature ne'er deserts the wise and pure;*

"Is that our key?" cried Ella.

"Looks like it," Christine Kennaway laughed. "Follow me and find out."

She disappeared back through the walled gateway and into the kitchen garden.

"If you don't come now," she called out, "you'll never know!"

Frank held onto Ella as she started to follow.

"No. I've got a bad feeling about this. I don't trust her."

"OK. What do we do, then?"

"Let's take the box and our spades and get out of here."

Frank put the ladder up against the wall, Ella grabbed the steel box and climbed over. Frank soon followed with the ladder and spades. As they ran towards the car, they could hear the voice of Christine screaming at them.

"You fools! You won't get away with it. It'll soon be Tar Barrel Night!"

"What does she mean? It's months away," puffed Ella as they jumped into their car and drove away.

"The letter again. Didn't Caleb say if we didn't complete this treasure hunt by Tar Barrel Night, then the company went to the Albanian Orphanage?"

"And she, literally, holds the key!"

As they drove through Ottery, Frank started laughing. Ella joined in without knowing why.

"We *are* complete fools!" chortled Ella.

"Don't I know it?" said Frank. "We're running away with a box containing our future and she's got the key!"

"Big deal. We can easily break into the box–it's only steel. I suggest we pop in to Kennaway Coopers tomorrow and get them to help us."

"Bingo!"

&

Next morning saw them walk into Kennaway Coopers with the blue steel box. They'd cleaned it up. It now looked almost brand new. They could now clearly see the small logo of Kennaway Coopers on the top.

"Hello, it's the treasure seekers!" Josiah Cobden called out.

"What have you got there?" Terence Talaton pointed at the steel box.

"That's our treasure and your future," replied Ella. "Unfortunately, we need a hammer or a locksmith to open it up."

"Bring it over here. I think I recognise the box," mused Terence. He took a closer look. "Yes, we had a batch of these made last year. We used to store some of our tools and parts. I put some of the bungs in one of them."

Josiah nodded. "They lock but the keys are all the same!"

"Have you got a key?" asked Ella.

"Yes, quite a few of them. They're in the spare key box in the main office. Hold on and I'll get one!"

The key was fetched, the blue steel box was opened, and Ella lifted out a small beer barrel.

"The head looks like it'll twist open," said Josiah.

It did and Ella gave the wooden head to Frank and took out a bundle of tightly rolled up papers.

"Bingo." Shouted Ella. "The jackpot!"

Frank unrolled the bundle and gave the top sheet to Ella. A group of workers had gathered around eager to see what would happen. Ella read out loud to the assembled throng:

"This letter is a legal agreement that signifies that the holder of this beer barrel and its contents is now the rightful owner of Kennaway Coopers. I, Caleb Kennaway, being of sound mind, do hand over all rights and responsibilities to the holder of this barrel.

Good luck and take good care of my baby!

Caleb Kennaway

Signed in the presence of Anthony Buckerell, solicitor, and Alice Aylesbeare, solicitor's secretary, the thirteenth day of November, the year of two thousand and eighteen."

"I think that's quite clear," said Josiah. "Say hello to our new owners!"

Tentatively, the workers moved forward and shook both Ella and Frank's hands. There was a buzz of conversation before Josiah held up his hand.

"Before we get carried away, there's work to be done. Our new owners will want to see that they can rely on us to keep the tradition of barrel making alive and well in Ottery."

"So back to work!" commanded Terence.

There was a nod of agreement and the workers went back to their areas and recommenced their interrupted tasks.

Josiah turned back to Frank and Ella. "Please follow us and we'll take you to the main office. George Snook will be wanting to know about this."

George Snook greeted them with a hearty handshake and bid them welcome. "Please take a seat and catch your breath."

Ella and Frank sat down. "I want you to know that both Frank, my husband, and I will be taking joint ownership. Until we understand a little bit more about how the company works, we will be very hands–off. A light touch, I think, is the phrase."

"I take it you want us to continue with Caleb's business plan?"

"Is it working? Is it a good plan?" asked Ella.

"Yes, and yes."

"Then keep on keeping on."

Frank and Ella spent another hour talking to John and the other two office staff. Right from the start, George Snook suggested that Terence and Josiah joined in with the discussions. Five became seven as tea and coffee were poured, biscuits nibbled and the topics flowed in a forthright but sincere manner.

"There's something I need to say but it's not very pleasant." Ella took a deep breath. "We both read in the local newspaper that Caleb was not very complimentary about the leadership skills of the management team."

"Yes, we read that as well," George Snook agreed.

"However," Terence added, "we had a good long look at ourselves. He was right. We relied on him to make all the decisions. We would go to Kenneth, he would go to Caleb and it would take an age for the simplest decisions to be implemented."

"Now, we have a meeting between the three of us and we ask ourselves a simple question– W.W.C.D?"

Frank laughed, "I know what that means. What would Caleb do?"

"Indeed! We don't take long to figure out the answer to that question. Then we implement it!"

"It's not let us down so far!" Josiah chortled.

Both Ella and Frank joined in with the laughter and nodded their heads.

"Exactly what we were hoping to hear!" said Ella.

Eventually, all that needed to be said was said. The new owners shook everyone's hands and then left with the contents of the beer barrel tucked safely away in the blue steel box. Terence gave Ella two identical keys.

"Just in case you lose one!" Ella locked the box and gave it to Frank. "My bodyguard!"

On the way home, Ella phoned Alice Aylesbeare: "Hi, Alice, are you at work? Good, can we drop some papers over to you? See you in about half an hour."

Frank and Ella asked Alice to make photocopies of the contents of the miniature beer barrel before depositing the originals in the safe at Buckerell's of Budleigh. "We'll take the photocopies with us, just in case anyone raises any doubts!"

They then went with Alice round to Earls in Budleigh Salterton and enjoyed a quiet relaxing cup of coffee.

"What a morning!" sighed Frank. "That's the treasure hunt out of the way. It's time we concentrated our minds on Caleb's murderer."

Alice was thoughtful. Ella asked, "What's wrong, Alice?"

"I remember witnessing that agreement with Anthony. Is it really such a long time ago?"

"Yes," considered Ella, "Such a lot has happened since that time."

They sat in judicious silence drinking their coffee.

"What are you going to do, Frank?" asked Alice.

He put down his cup and was about to answer when Ella jumped in. "It's time to bring in Sergeant Knowle and PC Hydon."

"Oh yes, now what did PC Hydon call it?"

"A touch of the Poirots?"

"As I recall, his exact words were," Ella stopped and twisting her face, she resumed with a strong Devon accent, "Why don't 'ee do a Pierrot?"

"We prefer *Murder in Paradise* but we're happy to cater to PC Hydon's little foibles."

≈≈

Elsie Knowle and Alf Hydon sat down in Frank and Ella's front room listening to the evidence, the theories and the plan to bring the murderer to justice.

"As far as I can see," summed up Elsie, "You've got four suspects. Christine is Caleb's wife and she was in the house all evening and all night as was Kenneth, Caleb's son. She has a horrendous temper, was capable of pushing her husband through the bannisters and is bitterly opposed to his decision to give away the company. Kenneth was so drunk that he thinks he may have pushed Caleb over the bannisters without being aware of it."

"Correct," said Frank.

"And Carl and Fabian were there during the evening and took part in the arguments. Carl went to a meeting and could have gone back to Kennaway Court after the meeting. Fabian did go back to Kennaway court to put Kenneth to bed and says he heard an argument in Caleb's bedroom."

Frank continued "They've all got motives to get rid of Caleb. Whether the motives are strong enough to actually go ahead and murder him is something we need to discover at the meeting."

Alf butted in. "It seems to me, you've not got much of a case. All four of them could be the murderer. How do 'ee sort this one out?"

"I want one of them to incriminate themselves," argued Frank. "They'll give themselves away if we go through the evidence."

"But a lot of it is circumstantial," answered Elsie.

"What about Kenneth's comments about Christine's lover?"

"It's still circumstantial," continued Elsie.

"I'd still like a meeting with them all. I'd also like to include the Zummerset Zyder mafia, Delbert, Norbert and Albert. They played some part in all the wheeling and dealing that was going on. Both Carl and Fabian told us they were planning to relocate the company in Taunton. And they were in Ottery on the night of the murder. And Christine was planning to buy Taunton Norton Cider. They're part of the motives. It all goes around in circles. Their presence might set off a discussion or argument that may incriminate our murderer."

"I'm not so sure about the evidence this time," considered Elsie, "By all means, have a meeting but I don't think we'll make it part of the official investigation. I'm happy to attend but in a civilian advisory capacity in plain clothes."

"Oi'll be there. Does that mean I can wear plain clothes as well?"

"Yes, Alf," said Elsie. "I'm happy to set up the meeting. Kennaway Court would be the ideal venue. Holding it on home turf may make our suspects overconfident. And overconfidence leads to mistakes. However, I think we'll need more evidence than this to be able to make an arrest."

"Do you think we should forget about a meeting?"

"We can't keep Kenneth's presence back in this country a secret for long. Let's strike while the iron's hot and see what happens.

Ella changed the subject by telling Elsie and Alf about the end of the treasure hunt.

"I hear you're the new owners of Kennaway Coopers?"

"Yes."

"Now, that's a good enough reason to have this meeting. There may be some fireworks. Someone may get burned. Let's hope it's one of our suspects!"

"Oi'm assuming 'ee don't mean real fireworks?" laughed Alf.

"Certainly not," replied Elsie.

Chapter Seventeen

Ah! well a-day! what evil looks
Had I from old and young!
Instead of the cross, the Albatross
About my neck was hung.

The meeting was organised for the following morning at Kennaway Court. "This is getting to be a tradition," exclaimed Sergeant Knowle.

Frank and Ella exchanged a smile and a knowing nod of their heads.

"Shall we get started?"

The elegant lounge of Kennaway Court had enough comfortable chairs to seat all of the invited guests.

Christine Kennaway occupied one of the comfortable armchairs.

Fabian Fassbender and Carl Copper sat side by side on the two-seater sofa.

The three representatives of the Taunton Norton Cider company, Norbert Fitzwarren, Delbert Fitzpaine and Albert Fitzhead sat opposite them on the larger Chesterfield sofa.

All had accepted Sergeant Knowle's invitation without too much dissent.

Ella and Frank sat side by side on the Love-seat. Sergeant Knowle sat by one of the two doors on a well-worn wooden chair and PC

Hydon parked himself on another wooden chair by the other door. Both police officers kept their promise to attend in plain clothes.

There was one unoccupied chair near the piano.

Frank stood up and consulted his clipboard.

"Thank you all for attending our little meeting this afternoon."

"As if we had any choice in the matter," remarked Fabian.

"Wouldn't miss one of your denouements," said Delbert with an exaggerated smile.

"We just wanted to bring you all up to date with matters."

Ella then stood up with a beaming, irrepressible face, "And to let you know about the culmination of our little treasure hunt."

"Yes!" PC Hydon piped up from his chair by the door. "All of you, bid a warm welcome to the new owners of Kennaway Coopers, Mr and Mrs Raleigh."

There were astonished looks from Carl and Fabian.

"But the key," stuttered Christine Kennaway.

"Now surely you didn't expect your husband to have the only key? After all, it's always good to have an alternative if something goes wrong! Eh, Mrs Kennaway?"

She looked stunned and angry.

"We've already taken over," announced Frank. "It's all legal and the workforce is very pleased to be staying here in Ottery!"

PC Hydon giggled, and Christine Kennaway turned to look at him with real hatred in her eyes. PC Hydon returned her stare with a gentle smile.

Ella sat down and Frank stood and took her place.

"Now, I'd like to take you back to the night of Caleb Kennaway's death," continued Frank, "We have come to the indubitable conclusion that someone in this room murdered Caleb Kennaway."

The proverbial pin didn't dare drop.

"But who," resumed Ella, "had a motive, the opportunity and the means to take Caleb's life?"

"Fabian Fassbender?"

"You wanted to sell the company lock, stock and barrel with the help of your backers, Fassbender Weissbier in Bavaria."

The interested parties in the room looked at him with astonishment.

"I cannot deny it."

"But would you kill to get control?" asked Frank.

"You were there when the arguments took place. And you were spotted on camera soon after the murder speeding through Cranbrook in your black Mercedes. PC Hydon spent some time finding you on the cameras."

"Did you push him down the stairs and then leave the scene of the crime in a hurry?"

There was silence as the whole room imagined the trail of events.

Frank took over. "And what about Carl Cooper? You wanted to sell the company. In fact, you wanted to sell it to anyone at any price. Or, at the very least, move the company out of the county away from Ottery. You also wanted to shut down Tar Barrel Night. Just like the others, you were part of the argument that evening and although people saw and heard you leave, who is to say that you didn't come back after your meeting and commit the crime?"

"Now we move on to the three gentlemen from the Taunton Norton cider company."

"Now, wait a minute. You can't be suggesting that we had anything to do with this altercation." Albert looked most put out.

"Actually, Mr Fitzhead, I was about to say that you three have the luxury of an indisputable alibi. At the time of Caleb's murder, you were caught on a camera on the M5 motorway."

"I always said they were a wonderful invention," Delbert Fitzpaine chirped in.

"Yes, that was twice that night, I believe" boomed PC Hydon.

"You were caught speeding on the motorway and near Ottery," Sergeant Knowle informed the trio. "Helps us to accurately locate you at vital times! The tickets are in the post, I believe!"

᎒᎒

Ella resumed centre stage. "Then there's the loving wife. Christine Kennaway. You wanted money. Desperately. You were part of the argument as well."

"Why did you want money?" Carl broke in, "You live in the lap of luxury."

"I think I can answer that," said Albert Fitzhead, "She wished to purchase the Taunton Norton Cider company. I think they call it moving on to bigger and better things!"

"You turned me down flat."

"An opening gambit. I'm sure you would have come back to us with a more acceptable offer."

"It was going to be our retirement fund!" said Delbert Fitzpaine with a twinkle in his eye.

"Retirement? But..." said Carl with some confusion in his voice.

"We're getting too old for this game," sighed Albert.

Ella continued. "But Mrs Kennaway wanted money as soon as possible."

"Why?" Christine Kennaway asked.

"Because...." a male voice began. The door beside Sergeant Knowle opened slowly and in walked Kenneth Kennaway.

☙❧

"But you're in jail? In Sarandë?" Christine Kennaway appeared genuinely dismayed. "Besa..." She chose not to complete her comment.

"I don't think so–unless I escaped and made my way halfway across Europe just to see you, dear mother! The prodigal son has returned!" Kenneth held his arms out in front of him as if preparing to hug her.

"Sit down, please, Mr Kennaway." Sergeant Knowle pointed to the spare chair by the piano.

"Yes, sorry." Kenneth stopped his prodigal son impression and took his place in the assembled company.

"As I was saying," continued Ella. "you wanted money not only to buy the Taunton Norton cider company, but also your Albanian lover and his charity were demanding your regular contribution."

"Lover?" said Kenneth in a mockingly shocked voice. "What would Daddy say?"

"Mr Kennaway, again would you kindly refrain from provocative comments!" asked Sergeant Knowle in a quiet but authoritative voice.

Ella once more continued, "You were part of the argument. In fact, you were a major part of the argument. And you were here in the house when everyone except your husband and son had gone."

Frank swapped places with Ella and turned towards Kenneth.

"Of course, Kenneth, you were in the house, rather the worse for wear. You argued with your father and then ran away when the situation got a bit too much for you."

"I thought I'd killed him!"

"I know, and you faked your death to avert suspicion. Unfortunately, you trusted the wrong man–Besart Clifteli."

"Clifteli!" exclaimed Christine.

"You recognise the name, Mrs Kennaway?"

"Er, no. Isn't Clifteli an Albanian musical instrument? Strange to be named after a musical instrument!"

"Mum! You needn't act in such a stupid misleading manner. I know who, or should I say what, Mr Clifteli is. I've seen the photo in his office."

"Oh no!" Christine's face lost some of its colour. "I don't understand? Why would you fake your death? All the grief you've given me." Christine Kennaway's voice faded away. She appeared to have drifted into a trance. "Unless… Kenneth. You killed him. You pushed my husband down the stairs and then just went to bed."

Frank moved into the middle of the room. "Yes, Mrs Kennaway. That's one way of looking at it. However, Kenneth was far too inebriated. He was drinking throughout the argument. Fabian, Mr Fassbender, had to carry him to his bedroom and leave him there to sleep it off."

"Whereas you," continued Ella, "played a major part of the argument. Even though you were preparing to leave your husband you spent the night in Kennaway Court. That gave you ample opportunity to push Caleb down the stairs. I assume the argument continued after everyone else had left. You put on your evening dress gloves once more so as to leave no fingerprints and pushed him to his death."

"No!"

Ella ploughed on. "Mrs Kennaway, we found your evening gloves in the compost bin in the garden, half-burnt. Sergeant Knowle took them away for analysis and found your DNA and your husband's DNA all over them."

"What's more," added Frank, "the forensic team found fibres from your husband's dressing gown on the gloves. Fibres transferred from his dressing gown to your gloves when you pushed him over the bannisters."

Mrs Kennaway stood up, steely resolve in her eyes. "You two little detectives are barking up the wrong tree. I didn't kill my husband. The DNA and fibres could have been transferred at any point during the evening. Husbands and wives do hug each other, you know. I was wearing my gloves before and after dinner. I burnt my evening gloves because they were an all too gruesome reminder of that horrible, horrible evening."

Frank and Ella were expecting some form of confession, not an upright rejection of their findings. The meeting was not turning out as planned.

Christine Kennaway was in full flow. "No, you're wrong. You can't prove a thing. Arrest me if you want to, Sergeant, but my solicitor will tear your case to shreds. Now, if you will excuse me, I'm going upstairs to get changed and then I'm going out for a walk."

"Before you go, mother dearest, there's a letter for you." Kenneth got up from his seat and handed her an envelope. "It's got an Albanian postmark. The postman gave it to me as I walked in."

With a flounce of her head, she took the letter from Kenneth and moved to the door. She stumbled slightly as she reached for the door handle. PC Hydon stood up as if to help her. She stared at him with a fixed expression. He opened the door and stood aside. Christine Kennaway turned back to the assembled company and smiled. To Ella's eyes, the smile appeared sinister and superior. She's got away with it, Ella thought.

༒

"What do we do now?" Ella quietly asked her husband.

There was no reason to keep the meeting going. Everyone started to make their excuses and exited the room. The Zummerset Zydermakers headed back to Taunton for an intense strategy discussion about the future of the company.

"We will not be selling our company to that woman," stated Albert, "If I know anything about people, I think you were absolutely correct with your conclusions. All you've got to do is prove it!"

Fabian Fassbender and Carl Cooper both got up to leave. They turned to Ella and Frank.

"She did it," said Carl. "I'm convinced she murdered her husband."

Fabian nodded in agreement and together they solemnly left the house. Frank watched them leave and climb into Fabian's Mercedes. Fabian didn't start the engine. They just sat there earnestly debating their futures.

Kenneth left the room and headed for the kitchen to make himself an all-day English breakfast–something he had heartily missed in his voluntary absence.

Not knowing what else to do, Frank and Ella gathered their papers together and retreated to their car. The two police officers followed them. "Let's retire to the London Arms, find ourselves a quiet corner and see where we go from here," said Sergeant Knowle in a gentle, understanding voice.

Chapter Eighteen

And I had done a hellish thing,
And it would work 'em woe:
For all averred, I had killed the bird
That made the breeze to blow.

The four of them were sat in the snug of the London Arms, the lunchtime crowd had dispersed, and they were able to talk in undisturbed peace.

"I felt sure that when she had heard all the evidence, she'd say something to give herself away," said Ella.

"I was hoping for an outright confession," remarked Frank. "All we got was egg on our faces!"

"Well, 'ee can't win them all," said PC Hydon. "You tried your best. At least, 'ee eliminated some of the others. At least, I think 'ee did." He scratched his chin in a puzzled manner. "The more I think about this case, the less I understand."

"Did you see her smile?" Ella whispered. "She knew we knew and yet she knew we couldn't prove a thing!"

The quietness was interrupted by the crackle of Sergeant Knowle's radio. She listened and then turned to PC Hydon. "Traffic Accident. They want us to attend. Come on."

They both rose to their feet. PC Hydon took a quick swig of his orange juice and re-attached his helmet onto his head.

"We'll be in touch," said Sergeant Knowle, "Soon." And with that, they were gone.

Frank and Ella sat there in silence. Suddenly, living in East Devon had lost some of its allure.

❦

I was driving to Ottery St Mary to visit my friend. She's quite old now and can't get out as much as she'd like. She lives in Yonder Close. I was going to take her to Otter Nurseries for a bite to eat and a look around.

It's a straight road here for quite a while and I could this person walking towards me. It looked like a lady and she was on the correct side of the road and I thought I didn't need to slow down. As I was about to pass her, she....

Take your time. Do you need a tissue?

No, I've got my handkerchief. I'm alright now. I need to tell you.

As I was about to pass her, she just stepped out into the road. Why? Why did she do that? I'll never forget the look on her face. She just stared like one of those zombies you see in the silly horror films.

I couldn't miss her. She hit the bonnet and sort of flew over the roof and landed in the road behind me.

I stopped the car. I had to. I got out and screamed at her. I think I asked her if she was OK. She wasn't. I could tell. I worked in hospitals before I retired. I knew she was dead or dying.

When I got to her side, there was blood coming out of her mouth. She had a piece of paper in her hands. It looked like a letter. I took it from her as I called you on my mobile.

She just lay there and mumbled "Those two little detectives were right!" I don't know what she meant. She closed her eyes and coughed up some more blood and just lay there.

I knew she was dead. What did she mean by "Those two little detectives were right?"

Oh, I think I know.

⁂

Frank drove Ella back to Otterbury. As they were pulling into their drive, Ella's mobile rang. She checked who it was and answered it. "Hello!"

"Switch your phone to speaker-phone so Frank can hear this." The solemn but distinctive tones of Sergeant Knowle filled the car.

"We've just finished at the Traffic Incident. Just outside Ottery. You'll never guess what's happened!"

Frank had stopped the car and turned off its engine.

"It's bad news, isn't it?"

"Every traffic accident is bad news, I suppose."

"It's Christine Kennaway, isn't it?"

"How did you guess?"

"You wouldn't be calling us otherwise."

"Good thinking! Anyway, she was out walking when she was hit by a car. The driver stopped. She's in a bad way."

"Who? Christine Kennaway?"

"No, the driver. She told me that Christine saw her coming and simply stepped out in front of her. She couldn't stop. She couldn't avoid hitting her. The driver stopped her car and ran back to help her."

"Christine Kennaway's dead?"

"Yes. As the driver was phoning for an ambulance, Christine Kennaway grabbed her hand, gave her a piece of paper and mouthed six words to the lady."

There was a brief silence on the other end of the phone.

"I bet the piece of paper was that letter that Kenneth gave her," said Frank.

"Correct!"

"And it was from the Albanian gentleman telling her it was all over."

"Correct, again. You're getting good at this!" Elsie's voice lifted and Frank could imagine her smiling. "He didn't want his charity to be involved with a murderer."

"But what about those six words?" shouted Ella, "Tell us. What did she say?"

"The lady driver said it sounded like 'Those two little detectives were right!'"

"I knew it," shouted Ella again. "It was that smile."

"What a horrible way of escaping justice," murmured Frank.

Chapter Nineteen

Joy, virtuous Lady! Joy that ne'er was given,
Save to the pure, and in their purest hour

"I don't see how Christine Kennaway could have kept us from taking over the company until Tar Barrel Night. That was months away."

"I think it was bravado. She was just out to scare you."

"Well, I'm looking forward to Tar Barrel Night but between then and now we've got some work to do."

Frank and Ella were sat in the main office at Kennaway Coopers for their monthly meeting with the management committee of George Snook, Kenneth Kennaway, Terence Talaton and Josiah Cobden.

"How are things?"

"Well, orders are up as you can see on your spreadsheet," announced George.

"The website and your targeted advertising in the local papers are paying dividends. Your interviews with those national magazines brought in some business," said Kenneth.

"Every barrel being used on Tar Barrel Night is made by us and is sponsored by us with all the local pubs."

"And the share offer to the workforce has been welcomed by everyone. We've just got to dot the tee's and cross the eye's and we'll be ready to announce it to the trade journals on Tar Barrel Night."

"The pay rise that goes hand in hand with the increased output is being considered."

"'Oi think they'll bite your hand off!"

"Any negatives?"

"Why didn't you two take this place over earlier!"

☙❧

November the Fifth, Tar Barrel Night, was an experience Frank and Ella were never to forget. The noise of the crowds, the smell of the burning tar, the sparks of flames whisking through and above the animated spectators. It was controlled chaos. Was this England or Dante's Inferno?

Terence and Josiah guided them through the crowds to the best viewing spots. Some of the workforce were stewarding the bustling event, one of two were amongst the carriers. Every one of them greeted Ella and Frank with a cheery smile and a respectful "Good evening, ma'am. Good evening, Frank!"

The tar filled barrels from Kennaway Coopers played their part as they were set alight and carried through the darkened, pedestrianised streets of Ottery St Mary.

Fifteen thousand people crowded into Yonder Street, Broad Street and Mill Street and then down to St Saviour's Bridge and onto the expanse of grassland beside the River Otter. In the centre of the grassland stood the bonfire of all bonfires awaiting the arrival of the remnants of the flaming tar barrels.

Generations of locals made up the elite groups chosen to carry the barrels. Each of the town's pubs sponsored a Kennaway barrel.

The evening had started off with children carrying smaller barrels followed by bigger barrels for the town's youths and women before the conclusion of the evening with the men's event. Their flaming barrels weighed almost five stone.

"You know, some of Devon's towns roll their barrels through the streets," shouted Josiah above the tumult. "We're the only town where we carry them!"

They stood aside as another barrel was lit outside the Rusty Pig and a brave, foolhardy warrior wearing fire-proofed gloves ran past them carrying the burning barrel on his shoulders.

"Wasn't that Kenneth?" yelled Frank.

"It's his first year," bellowed Josiah, "Hopefully not his last!"

They watched him pass the barrel onto another runner and he stood there as bystanders and strangers applauded and slapped him on the back. Ella was delighted to see the elated, satisfied expression on his sweaty face.

They made their way with the excited throng down to St Saviour's Bridge and cheered with everyone else as the bonfire was lit and fireworks shot up into the starry night sky.

As the flames of the bonfire started to dwindle, one corner of the crowd started to sing. Line by line others in the huge crowd joined in:

> *Sweet-breathing kine,*
> *The old grey Church,*

The curfew tolling slow,
The glory of the Western Sky,
The warm red earth below.
O! Ottery dear! O! Ottery fair!
My heart goes out to thee,
Thou art my home, wher'er I roam,
The West! The West for me!

Thank you for reading The Ottery Lottery.

If you want to help spread the word about the book, then I'd really appreciate it if you left a review on the Amazon book page. Please do it NOW!

All the chapter heading quotes are taken from the poems of Samuel Taylor Coleridge.

To receive up to date information about the East Devon Cosy Mysteries please sign up for our irregular newsletter. You'll receive 6 walks in and around Sidmouth, an eBook that includes the walks Ella and Frank enjoyed in Cidered in Sidmouth.

To subscribe and to find out more about Frank and Ella Raleigh and their East Devon Cosy Mysteries please visit the author's website www.eastdevoncosymysteries.com

The author, PA Nash, can also be reached on:-

Facebook – https://www.facebook.com/pa.nash.182

Twitter – https://twitter.com/PANash49873070

Pinterest – https://www.pinterest.co.uk/EastDevonCosyMysteries/

or by

Email – info@eastdevoncosymysteries.com

You've been reading the third book in the East Devon Cosy Mysteries series.

The first book in the series, Cidered in Sidmouth, involved newly retired Frank and Ella Raleigh finding an unexpected surprise when they went to deliver a wrongly delivered package. WPC Knowle called it a tragic accident, Frank and Ella didn't agree. Guess who was right?

The second book called The Dudleys of Budleigh, begins with a note sent to Anthony Buckerell that read "In the seventh hour of the night on the seventh day of the year you will die." At 7.59, surrounded by police in a windowless locked cell, he did. How? Ask Dudley.

THE SECOND BOOK IN THE EAST
DEVON COSY MYSTERY SERIES

The Dudleys of Budleigh

P.A.NASH

All the books in this series are available now at Amazon on kindle and in paperback

The fourth book in the series will be available early in 2020.

Acknowledgements

Many of the places mentioned in this book do exist. Some of the places exist only in the figment of my imagination. I'll leave it to you to come to East Devon and Ottery St Mary in particular to find out which are which.

Dedication

To the whole Nash family–

from Elsie's Bow to Resource Angel.

Love from PA.

The Pixies' Parlour Circuit

1. *Starting at St Saviour's Bridge, head 200 yards south to the Millennium Bridge.*

St Saviour's Bridge was built originally by Bishop Grandisson in the mid-14th century. Several have since been swept away by flooding. The latest bridge was built in 1851 and widened in 1992. It is named after a chapel, dedicated in 1355, built by the bridge but demolished in the 1540s. The new millennium bridge was built as a commemoration in 2000.

2. Cross the bridge and turn right to the waymarker on top of the flood bank. Follow the path to the next footbridge over a back run of the river. Cross the bridge and turn right up to the gate and waymarker on the skyline. Follow the path along the cliff edge above the river and take the next path-gate on your right. Follow the path down through the woods to Pixies' Parlour.

Pixies Parlour, a tiny cave in the soft sandstone cliffs that border the floodplain at this point, is now a hallowed monument to Samuel Coleridge Taylor's youthful poetic spirit. A visit to Pixies Parlour in 1793, was spun into the poem–Songs of the Pixies.

3. Continue past Pixies' Parlour to the gate in the fence. Follow the hedge on your left to the field gate, then bear left and upwards along the wide track towards the lake on your left. Pass the lake on your left and continue to the road.

The lake is artificial probably constructed in the medieval period to supply freshwater fish to Knightstone Manor.

4. Carefully cross the Sidmouth road and continue up Knightstone Road for about 150 yards later ignoring the road that turns left into Knightstone Farm. Turn right at a waymarker up into a field.

5. When you reach the top of the bank into the field, stand facing the solitary oak tree in the middle of the field to the south. The path is not always well defined here if the field is under crops, but it runs in a direct line to the fingerpost and stile on the opposite side. Past the stile, keep the hedge on your immediate right.

6. Reaching the road, turn right. Reaching the outskirts of Wiggaton look for a footpath on your left. The path leads along two sides of a square back to the Sidmouth road.

7. Immediately before reaching the road, turn sharp left up another footpath and follow it past some farm buildings. After the farm buildings turn right down another path, called Lancercombe Lane, back again to the Sidmouth road.

8. At the road, turn right for a few yards, cross the road and follow another path down through a field to the River Otter. Follow the path in a southerly direction towards Tipton St John.

9. Pass through a group of factory buildings and turn right past the mill to the bridge. Cross the bridge.

Parts of the mill appear to be Tudor in origin with many later additions and alterations. The building is still in private ownership. Look out for a new green energy installation–an Archimedes screw turbine which now supplies electricity to the Mill.

10. Turn right and follow the river upstream to Tipton Mill Weir. and within a couple of hundred yards came upon another concrete construction.

This is a weir built to power the watermill. Engineered with banking on the riverside with many tons of heavy rocks. The head of water is now put to work again producing green energy whilst the rush and twist of the river overruns the huge stone damn.

11. Follow the footpath as it runs parallel to the River Otter back to Ottery St Mary.

Look out for hollows and ditches in the fields. These were carved out by the River Otter as it shifted its course quite rapidly over time. The old river courses can be found crossing and re-crossing the floodplain in dozens of places. As you approach Ottery, the path again joins the old Sidmouth branch railway line. The railway arrived in Ottery in 1874 with a branch from Tipton St John to Budleigh Salterton added in 1897. It closed in 1967.

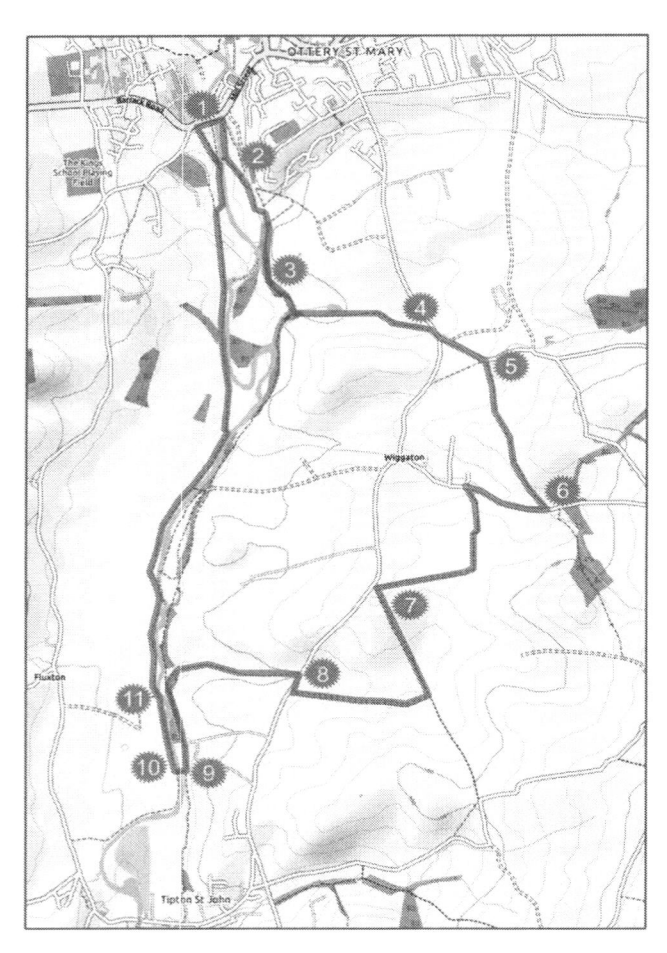

About the Author

PA Nash and his supportive wife moved to glorious East Devon nearly a decade ago having taken early retirement from his previous job in South East England. Not quite ready for a life of endless relaxation, PA has since dabbled as a website administrator for the South West Coast Path, an IT office assistant in a local school and a Wordpress website designer. This is his first cosy mystery book.

I've read so many cosy mystery novels in the past ten years. Some series like MC Beaton's Hamish Macbeth and Agatha Raisin were excellent, others not so!

I thought I could put together a series based around an area of England. Everyone's written about the Cotswolds and the Midsomer counties, so I thought it would be best to avoid those areas. We live in a beautiful part of the South West of England. East Devon is full of quaint villages, relaxing towns, peaceful countryside and hidden gems. It's just waiting for a few juicy murders! The police presence is minimal. The population is not as full of old-aged pensioners as some would have you believe. Perhaps it's time to create a rival to Midsomer!

I enjoy walking so I've made use of the South West Coast Path and other footpaths in my books. Each book will have a selection of walks most reasonably fit people can complete. Some of the walks can be found on the excellent South West Coast Path Association's website.

I intend to create a series of short cosy mysteries based around the towns and villages of East Devon.

Cidered in Sidmouth

Frank and Ella made their debut appearance in Cidered in Sidmouth, the first book in the East Devon Cosy Mystery series. Here's an excerpt from the early chapters:

CHAPTER ONE

You've ruined everything. How dare you think you can get away with it.

The vase was within reach. Picking it up in anger with no thought for the consequences, it was a simple and automatic action to crash it down on his head. The man stumbled backwards, ricocheted off the single armchair in the room and fell head first on the stone floor.

There was silence. Not even a moan.

I've killed him.

Chapter Two

The postman took 3 hours to deliver a giant roll of bubble wrap. Someone told him, "pop it in the corner."

Retirement is wonderful, Frank thought. No more pressure and stress. No more looking at the clock. No more living by other people's expectations. No more... well, everything.

Now, there's time to while away. Old friends to greet, new friends to meet. Time to enjoy the pleasure of enjoying time well spent. Like today. The autumn sun was lighting up the top of the trees, there was a breeze to just keep it this side of cool, the leaves were floating sporadically to the moist earth and Frank and Ella were strolling with another couple, Bella and George, friends from the village. They were heading through the woods along the old railway track from the Bowd down towards Harpford.

"Couldn't have done this ten years ago."

"No, we would've been too busy mollycoddling teachers," Ella smiled, "and then endlessly trying to see the best in children."

"Yes, rather than seeing the best of each other and this glorious countryside."

Frank never regretted for one nanosecond taking early retirement and moving down here to East Devon. Particularly on a carefree day like today.

"Autumn is definitely one of the best four seasons." Bella sighed.

They crossed over the East Devon Way footpath and followed the old railway track down to Knapp's Lane. Here they branched off to the right and ambled back over the stone bridge and into the pretty village of Harpford. They walked past the medieval church of St Gregory the Great. Crossing the River Otter by the rickety metal bridge, they trudged through the muddy field that led back to the Recreation Ground car-park. Here they bid each other farewell and both couples headed for their village homes.

Ella had enjoyed the walk and the companionship of their two friends. Retirement is wonderful. Except… you need a routine. You need something to live for. A reason to get up in the morning. You need interests and enthusiasms. At the moment, Ella wasn't totally sold on retirement.

⁂

At home, hidden somewhat obviously beside the green garden waste bin, was a small brown paper package that wouldn't fit through their letterbox. Ella picked it up before heading indoors. They made their usual cups of coffee and tea before Ella went to open the package. She wasn't expecting a delivery because she had bought nothing online in the last week. Ella stopped and examined the writing on the front.

"They've done it again. Almost the right address, totally the wrong location."

Living in River Street, Otterbury caused no end of problems to the jolly postmen at the local sorting office. They were forever getting mail intended for River Street in Sidmouth. Most of the time, Ella just underlined the postcode and put it back in the post-box down by the war memorial.

This time the autumnal sunshine was promising to continue, and Sidmouth was a wonderful place in which to wander around. Being out of season, you could park the car without too many problems.

"Why don't we find out where this doppelganger lives?"

Frank put down the local paper. "What are you talking about?"

"This package. It's not for us. It should be for River Street in Sidmouth."

"Not again. Surely someone must be able to read in the Post Office. This never used to happen when we were in Kent. Well, not as often."

"They sort it by machine these days, Frank!"

"Well, they ought to sort it out. Can I see how they messed it up this time?"

Frank took the package before bursting into laughter.

"They haven't even got the number correct. Look, it says 23. Since when have we lived at 23? The sorting machine can't read. 23 is an age I'd love to be once again, but it's nowhere near our address."

"If you were 23, then we wouldn't have been married all these years!"

"Right, scrub my last comment. Where was it posted?"

"Postmarked Cullompton."

"Local post office sorters should know better. Surely they know this is not Sidmouth?"

"I suppose the sorting machine could have mistaken the postcode for ours."

"It's written so scruffily. Someone was in a hurry." Frank put the package back down on the table.

"I'm going to phone the sorting office in Sidmouth about this. It happens all too often."

The automated phone message told them that this call may be recorded for monitoring and training purposes. Then Frank was connected to a gentleman who took their name and address, the details of the package and apologised for the mis-delivery. He suggested taking the package to the nearest post office and asking them to post it to the correct address. Then before Frank could vent any amount of scorn upon the Post Office, the line went dead. Frank stared at the phone before putting it down on its stand.

Ella watched his face become even more thunderous.

"Frank, you need to calm down. It's most unlike you. Let's have dinner and then we'll go into Sidmouth this afternoon, deliver the package to the correct address, have a walk along the seafront and grab an ice cream at Taste."

Taste was one of Sidmouth's secret delights. The best ice cream outside of Cornwall with a multitude of flavours and always exceedingly generous portions.

Frank visibly relaxed. "Good plan. Who'd have thought we'd be eating ice cream at the seaside in October."

Sidmouth had a reputation in some circles as the regency preserve of the elderly and infirm. Today that appeared to be so true as evidenced by the ponderous speed of much of the traffic. The ten-minute journey took well over double the usual time. The sunny weather was more like June than October. It had brought tourists and elderly locals out onto the streets. In the High Street, two large cars were attempting to reverse into spaces in which only a motorbike could safely park. The result was gridlock. Frank eventually was able to turn off left and sidle into the car park that only the locals know. He was grateful to find a space. They paid for an hour at the ticket machine and were soon nimbly dodging the dawdling crowds in their quest to find 23, River Street.

"It's so busy today." Ella had to shout as a muddy quad bike with an even muddier trailer zoomed up the narrow road past them. Ella stared at it as it roared around the corner.

There were houses with numbers and no names, houses with names but no numbers and a couple with neither names nor numbers. They were interspersed with a couple of shops that had names but never any numbers.

A group of cyclists travelling three abreast, passed them by. The group included two couples on bright red and orange tandems. Ella smiled at them and called out "Lovely afternoon!"

They all looked at her with disdain and carried on holding up a queue of cars behind them. Ella raised her eyebrows. "All sorts out today!"

Eventually, they found what appeared to be the right address. It was the end house of a terrace– a small trio of mellow red brick Edwardian dwellings. Frank called them two up, two downs. Ella called them quaint. Next door, separated by a walled alleyway, was The Mariner pub.

"I didn't know this pub was here. I've never heard of it before."

"Doesn't look too grand. Could be one to explore in the future." Frank added as he opened the black rusting metal gate that led up a short, uneven flagstone path.

The blue painted door was flanked by two flowerpots. Both had the remains of last year's annuals. Ella could not find a bell, so she knocked gently on the door. No-one answered.

"Can't we just leave the package on the doorstep and go for our ice-cream?" she said.

"Knock again–but louder."

Ella did so with the same result.

"If this were Otterbury, then someone would have left the key underneath the flowerpot," Frank chuckled.

"But it's not… This is Sidmouth."

"No harm in checking." Frank knelt down and lifted up the right-hand flowerpot and looked underneath.

"I don't believe it!" whispered Ella.

Frank picked up a sturdy looking latchkey and tried it in the lock. The key turned, the door opened, and Frank stuck his head inside before calling out. "Hello, anybody home? We've got a package for you!"

No-one answered.

"Hello?" repeated Frank.

"Just leave it on the doormat!" Ella was pleased that no-one was home. It would avoid a discussion about the Post Office, or even worse, the incorrect addressing of too much post these days. They would now just deposit the package and head off towards the seafront.

Frank had other ideas. Taking the package from Ella, he disappeared into, what he assumed to be, a hallway. He put it down on a small circular table hidden behind the front door.

"Wait a minute. I'm going to leave a note with the package. Have you got a pen and paper?"

Ella shook her head.

"Well, in that case, I'm just going to find something to write on in one of the rooms. I'll be straight back."

He called out again, "Hello, anybody in?"

There was no reply. As he ventured further into the house, Ella called out to him, "I'm not staying out here in full view of the suspicious Sidmouth public. I'm coming in as well!"

Frank casually walked into the front room. Ella looked around to see if anyone nearby was watching them and then quickly followed.

The room was dark, sparsely furnished and unkempt. A stone floor, a single battered old sea-blue armchair and a couple of stacked wooden chairs. No television, the remains of a coal fire in a dirty grate. The curtains were half open, but the windows were opaque with smudges of dirt. On the mantelpiece was a photo of a man and a woman, smiling lovingly at each other.

Getting accustomed to the lack of light, they could both see that someone had been having a severe disagreement. A coffee table lay overturned with its magazines and newspapers scattered on a threadbare rug. Two cushions from the armchair were also on the stone floor by the fireplace. Ella bent to pick one up and immediately jumped back with a startled "Oh! Frank, come here. Is this blood on the floor? Here, by the fireplace."

Frank had just opened the door leading to a back room which appeared to be a kitchen. Before he went in, he turned back towards Ella to examine the patch. Picking the other cushion off the floor, he let out a similar cry.

"You're right. It certainly looks like blood. Put the cushions back, exactly where you found them. Let's check out the rest of the house."

Ella hastily replaced the cushions and stepped around the scattered papers and magazines before following Frank into the kitchen. From here, they could see a sight they would take them a very long time to forget.

"Ella, have you got your phone with you?"

The back door was open and, in full view, on the right-hand side of the tiny paved and gravelled courtyard stood a huge wooden Cider Vat. It was quite the largest barrel that either had ever seen. Sticking out from the top of the vat were two bare legs.

Printed in Great Britain
by Amazon